ABOUT LAST NIGHT

THE MORGAN ERICKSSON SERIES
BOOK ONE

ANGELA M. JOHNSON

ISBN: 979-8-9856334-8-1 (paperback)
ISBN: 979-8-9856334-5-0 (e-book)

Angela M. Johnson
Prairie Grove, AR

For those one-night standers and walk of shamers: walk your walk, but leave that shame for someone else.
Do you, but do it unapologetically.

CONTENT WARNING

Some of the themes in this story may not be suitable for all, and as such, read with caution.

This book has graphic intercourse scenes (FM, FMM, and FMMM), SA, alcohol and drug use (consensual and non-consensual).

CHAPTER 1

NEVER AGAIN

"**M**organ, wait!" Eric called out as he sprinted down the hallway behind her. "Morgan!"

She turned on him quickly, fully prepared to release the rage that was building inside of her, but instead faced him with extreme calm. "Why Eric? Why should I wait? I have seen everything I needed to know how to appropriately respond. So, no, I will not wait. I'm done," she spat, turning around and walking away, her heels clicking loudly as she stomped down the corridor.

"So that's it then? Five years and you just walk away from me?" he cried aloud, his voice booming as it echoed down the hall.

"No, Eric," she sneered, turning to face him. "I am not walking away from you. I am running. A hundred miles an hour in the opposite direction," she said, pointing to the outer door. "And not a moment too soon. I just wish I would have seen this sooner," she said, motioning toward him.

The scent of whiskey wafted, accosting her nostrils with each huff as he breathed out heavily. "I made a mistake, Morg. I'm drunk and it just happened," he pleaded. "C'mon. You can't seriously break up with me. It's our engagement party."

She hated it when he called her that. Hated when he pouted. He always looked so pitiful and she would end up forgiving him. But not this time. No, the line he crossed, the damage he caused, could not be undone.

"You must think I'm an idiot," Morgan stated, crossing her arms. "Yes, it is our engagement party and despite that fact, I just found you making out with one of Melissa's friends. So please tell me again how I am the one throwing our five-year relationship away?"

Melissa was Eric's sister and over the last five years, she and Morgan had become very close. So when they announced their engagement, Melissa was beyond ecstatic. She couldn't wait to welcome Morgan into the family. Honestly, after five years, Melissa already considered her a member.

Just then, Melissa turned the corner and began swaying down the hallway toward the restrooms, coming upon Morgan and Eric. She stopped, looked at Morgan as she stood leaning against the far wall with her arms crossed and Eric, who stood an arm's length away with his hands on his hips, shifting his weight anxiously.

"What's going on," Melissa slurred.

"It's nothing," Eric said, turning away, unwilling to meet his sister's gaze.

"What the fuck did he do?" she accused, looking to Morgan for an answer.

"Just forget about it, Liss. Morg and I are just working through some things," Eric said avoidantly.

"Morg?" Melissa pleaded. "What's going on?"

"I can't do this," Morgan said, throwing her hands down in exasperation as she turned and walked back toward the St. Anthony ballroom.

Morgan Ericksson and Eric Watkins were having their engagement party at the Nicollet. They had attended one of Morgan's coworker's wedding and reception there last year where they had the time of their lives. The ambiance, the stained-glass windows, and the antique details made her fall in love with the venue. And after Eric proposed to her, they agreed their engagement party, and eventually their wedding, should be held there. They had good memories there, until now.

Morgan was a catering manager at a hotel in Minneapolis where they lived. She spent her entire life in Minnesota. That is where she had seen herself years into the future. A couple of kids and a small house in the suburbs with Eric. Who wouldn't want a life like that? But it's amazing how quickly all her hopes and dreams came crashing down around her. How one moment destroyed all that imagery. How one act of stupidity could forever alter her view of love and relationships. But it did. In that moment, she was forever altered.

Morgan didn't come from much. Her family wasn't well off like Eric's was, but she didn't consider them to be poverty stricken, either. She was an only child who grew up on the West Bank of Minneapolis in Riverside. Raised by a single mother who most times worked two jobs, sometimes three, to make ends meet. Her father had left when she was three, never to be heard from again. To be honest, he was probably a resident of Oak Park Heights. Living his days in Stillwater, surrounded by three walls and bars. Penance for his many years of nefarious acts upon the world.

When Morgan turned eighteen, she had thought about

looking him up, but eventually decided against it. What good would that do? What could he offer she didn't already possess? Definitely not closure or an explanation. She needed neither.

Her mom had done the best she could and, for the most part, raised her to be a good, kind-hearted individual. But this, the events of this night, would harden her. Would change her outlook on relationships and men forever. And why shouldn't it? Just another man who let her down. Just another man that proved that trusting people, especially with your heart, was a mistake.

Walking into the dining room, the guests stood and began clapping, turning to look where Morgan just entered.

Eric's mother, Elizabeth, walked over to Morgan, smiling that fake smile she was known for and pulled her into an embrace as she whispered in her ear, "Where is my son?" She released Morgan, continuing to smile for the guests, and placed her hand on Morgan's lower back as she ushered her back to the head table, muttering under her breath to her husband, "It's time for the toast."

Eric's father, Malcolm, stood, straightened his suit jacket, and twisted his cufflinks anxiously as he looked toward the door for his son.

The door opened and everyone turned, beginning to stand as Melissa walked in. She stopped in her tracks, scanning the room nervously until her eyes met Morgan's. She huffed a sigh of relief and then walked hesitantly to the head table, stopping in front of her father. She whispered something to Malcolm that Morgan could not make out, and Elizabeth turned her eyes suspiciously on Morgan as Malcolm departed the ballroom.

"What have you done?" Elizabeth whispered accusingly.

"What has she done?" Melissa countered in astonishment. "How about you ask what your asshole son has done?"

"Lower your voice, Melissa. Someone will hear you," Elizabeth uttered, maintaining her fake smile for the onlookers.

"Let them hear me! Excuse me, everyone," she announced loudly, tapping her knife against her champagne flute.

The guests all turned their attention to Melissa as they awaited the toast they assumed would follow.

"Yes. Thank you all for coming, but I apologize. My sorry excuse for a brother has done it again. That's right, folks. Like so many of the things he has been gifted in this pampered life of his, he has ruined it. He has ruined it, right?" Melissa asked, turning her attention to Morgan.

Morgan just nodded.

"Precisely. So,..." she said, turning back to the crowd, "this evenings' festivities are cut short. I apologize. But uh, the engagement is off. Thank you all for coming and please, take a to-go plate. I don't want all this boujee food to go to waste. Cheers," she said, raising her glass, chugging it down and slamming it on the table before walking around the table to embrace Morgan. "I'm sorry Morgs."

"I love you Melissa," Morgan said, smiling.

"Just 'cause he fucked up doesn't mean you don't still have me," Melissa assured her, sitting down in the chair next to her. She leaned into Morgan, resting her head on her shoulder. "Bitches for life?"

"Absolutely," Morgan insisted, squeezing Melissa tightly.

⌐LIVE•⌐

Pace. Remember your pace. Focus on your breath, in through your nose, and out through your mouth. Why am I struggling to focus today? Oh, shut up and just run!

Morgan ran down Grand Street after leaving the lofts. She passed in front of the hotel and crossed the bridge over the river, picking up the Principal Riverwalk and the John Pat Dorrian Trail on the other side; her normal five-mile route that started and ended at the downtown lofts where she now lived.

She had never been overly athletic in Minneapolis, but now that she was in Des Moines, she had to find a way to clear her head. A way to drown out all the chaos that danced about in the front of her mind. To drive away the intrusive thoughts that plagued her. Thoughts of Eric and their failed relationship. Of his betrayal and how quickly the people that were going to be her family became strangers. All of them except Melissa, that is. At least in the breakup, she got to keep Melissa.

Speaking of Melissa.

Morgan pressed the side of her earpiece, connecting with the call ringing in her ear.

"What's up, bitch!" Melissa screeched, causing Morgan to cringe as her voice boomed through her earbuds.

"Hello to you, too," Morgan replied.

"It's loud out. Where are you?"

"I'm running down along the river. What's up?"

"Can't I just call to check in on my main squeeze?"

"Of course you can. Anytime, in fact. How's your day going so far?"

"Fine. Just had another knock down drag out with Lizzie Borden over here." Melissa harrumphed.

Melissa and Eric's mother Elizabeth Anne Watkins, or "Lizzie Borden" as Melissa referred to her, was a pretentious, overbearing, busy body who loved to stick her nose in every aspect of her children's business whenever the opportunity arose for her to do so. Today's interference, as reported by Melissa, was regarding her having a date for her cousin Miranda's wedding next month.

"She had the nerve to suggest I ask Robert to escort me. To escort me!" she said, raising her voice. "As if I am unable to attend solo. As if I need a chaperone or that somehow a man's presence is required. You know what we should do?"

"No, but I am sure you are going to tell me." Morgan huffed as she pushed through the last leg of her run.

"Take the weekend off and come be my date." Melissa giggled.

"How about no," Morgan stated dryly.

"Can't you just imagine the looks on everyone's faces?"

"Yes, Liss. I can. Which is why I shall not be attending. Thanks for asking, but I am going to sit this one out."

"C'mon, Morgs!" Melissa pouted. "You're no fun, you know that?"

"So I've been told," Morgan answered.

Standing at the corner as she waited for the crossing light to blink green, she looked down at her watch as she reviewed her time and heart rate.

"Liss, can I call you back later? I am about to head up and will lose you in the elevator. Check back in at lunch?"

"Bitch," she trailed off exaggeratedly. "Fine! If you must go."

"I must."

"Think of me in the shower?" Melissa teased.

"I always do." Morgan chuckled.

She crossed the street and jogged the remaining block toward her building. As she neared the entrance, she saw a man exiting. She called out to him, "Hold the door, please!" Her key was attached to her shoelace, and she'd hoped she could just slide in behind him.

This mystery man made eye contact, looked her up and down, and then smirked as he shut the door behind him.

Morgan stopped in her tracks, shocked at how obvious the man had been in his disregard for her request.

He jogged across the street, hopped into an all-black Range Rover with tinted windows, and drove away.

Of course! Just another self-absorbed pretty boy living downtown with no care for the struggles of others. Just another Eric, this world would be better without.

"Asshole!" she muttered aloud as she bent down to untie the key from her shoelace so she could finally enter the building.

CHAPTER 2
CUE THE ASSHOLE

Jamison Elijah Masters. That was the name of the resident of the penthouse at the lofts where Morgan now lived in downtown Des Moines. The name that went with the face she could not get out of her head, along with the image of him smirking as he knowingly closed the door on her earlier that day; an act that solidified what his appearance alone had already told her—he was an asshole.

Morgan was on her hands and knees with a toothbrush, vigorously scrubbing the tile floors of her bathroom as another bout of intense cleaning was brought on by frustration. That was her norm. That was her reaction to getting irritated. She didn't get mad, raise her voice, or scream. She would just hyper fixate on deep cleaning and take all her frustrations out on every surface of her apartment as she purged every "unnecessary" item from her life. And as she would bag them up and toss them away, so too went her anger along with them. The OCD was strong with this one.

It had been almost six months since Morgan first arrived in

Des Moines, five since she had moved into the lofts, and yet some-how, today of all days, fate ruined her mood by placing Jamison Masters in her path. Just a rock to trip her up as she kept pace on her run route that day. The same route she had run time and time again, and yet, not once had their paths ever crossed before.

So why now?

Why was she being punished now? What had she done that was so terrible that the fates saw fit to torture her with this man who immediately induced flash backs of Eric?

This is not good! This will not do. I can't let him in again. I won't let him in again.

Morgan had worked so hard to wipe the pain of her and Eric from her mind. At first, she thought that the end of their relation-ship would mean she would lose her best friend in the process, but Melissa had chosen her. Despite the years together and the bond of family, Melissa stayed true to Morgan. She had her back. And why shouldn't she? Morgan did nothing wrong. She's not the one who had her tongue down Emma's throat mere feet away from the ballroom where their engagement was being celebrated. It was Eric; it had always been Eric. Despite their years together and the love she felt for him, something just always seemed off.

Being in a relationship with Eric was like going into the grocery store for two items. You didn't grab a cart or a basket because it was just two items. Then, before you knew it, your arms were full of the things you thought you needed, but that you were struggling to carry. That is what it felt like to be dating Eric. One by one, the items piled up until you realized this is just too much for any one person to carry.

Who is this Jamison Masters and why, oh why, is he such an asshole? Morgan thought as she scrolled through her social media looking for him.

Victor Saucedo lived on Morgan's floor, and knew everything

about everyone in the building, it seemed. He had provided her with a name to put with that face and the place where she now placed her hatred. It was a common name, but there was only one pompous, dark-haired, pretty boy without a single hair out of place on the screen in front of her now.

He even dresses like an asshole. High fashion and named brand everything, vacations on Martha's Vineyard, and Monte Carlo. Everything about him screams out "trust fund baby." And the more I scroll, and the harder I look, the evidence supporting that moniker just keeps piling up.

All black, tricked out, custom Range Rover; check. Daddy and mommy look like they're sponsored by Mattel as much plastic as there is between them; double check. Every caption of every photo read like the line from the staff meeting in "How to lose a guy in 10 days," surprisingly upbeat; the trust fund baby trifecta. Wealth, affluence and zero clue how hard the rest of the world had to work just to make ends meet, and every ingredient necessary so, *you, too, could create an asshole in just three easy steps*, her thoughts echoed in a jovial game show host's voice.

"Why do you want to know who this guy is so bad?" Victor asked, looking over Morgan's shoulder as she sat on her couch with her tablet in her lap.

"Call it insurance," Morgan said as she continued to scroll.

"Insurance of what?"

"That I will be none of the places he is. If I don't frequent the same establishments, there's no chance of having to socialize with him," Morgan explained.

"Well, it just so happens I would like to socialize with you sometime, so where should I frequent?"

"You shouldn't," she said flatly.

"Oh... uh," Victor stammered.

"I am so sorry. That came out entirely wrong. What I meant to say is, I don't socialize. I go out for work and have little to no time for fun. I am still getting to know my way around, so casual hang-outs aren't really in my wheelhouse."

"No, I get it. Perfectly understandable," Victor said, clearing his throat as he attempted to hide his true feelings. "Well, thanks for the glass of wine, but I should probably go."

"No. Thank you," Morgan said, not looking up from her tablet as Victor walked to the door.

As Victor walked out, Olivia Andrews, who was just about to knock, walked in. "Hello," Olivia flirted as Victor nervously closed the door behind him as he left. "Okay. What was that all about?"

"Oh, him? He's something else," Morgan replied. "He lives down the hall."

"What did you do to him?" she accused.

"Me? I did nothing," Morgan said defensively. "Why?"

"Because that man looked like you just kicked his puppy."

"Seriously, Olivia? Just go give him a hurt feelings report and I'll deal with it later."

"Ouch. That was cold, Morgs."

"Please!" she shouted. "Sorry. Don't call me that," Morgan finished.

"Never again," Olivia mumbled, crossing her heart in jest.

Olivia Andrews worked at the hotel with Morgan as the lounge manager, and, as soon as she'd arrived, immediately established herself as Morgan's partner in crime.

The first month Morgan lived in Des Moines, she stayed at the hotel. As she got a place to live lined up, and all her belongings delivered from Minneapolis, Olivia ensured she made introduc-tions on Morgan's behalf to every bartender and hostess downtown.

"Getting things done around here requires know how. And by know how, I really mean it's all about who you know. You know?

So I plan to introduce you to anyone who's anyone," Olivia gushed.

Olivia scheduled meet and greets at every cocktail hour, hors d'oeuvres at the country club, and rounds of golf with every finance bro in town, hoping to get Morgan connected.

After hearing Morgan's tragic story about her engagement party, Olivia had made it her mission to find Morgan a boyfriend.

One afternoon, while Olivia and Morgan were at lunch, Olivia pried. "You're into boys, right?"

"Boys, no. Men, yes."

"What about women?"

"I've never had the pleasure. So I don't rightfully know," she admitted.

"Don't knock it until you try it," Olivia said, fanning herself. "Best orgasms ever. Hands down. Pun intended." Olivia giggled.

"Dumbass." Morgan chuckled. "I wasn't knocking it. I just said I have never done it." Morgan took a sip of her drink, the ice cubes clinking as she sat it down.

"Oh, but you should," Olivia said, taking another sip of her wine.

"The girl, should what?" interrupted Uriel.

"Ooh. Morgan, Uriel. Uriel, Morgan." Olivia pointed back and forth as she made the introductions.

"Charmed, I'm sure," Morgan teased as she attempted a southern accent, putting out her hand to be kissed.

"Well, I do declare," Uriel said, kissing Morgan's hand and then pretending to faint into the booth beside Olivia. "A woman after my own heart."

"Isn't he fabulous?" Olivia boasted as she snuggled up to Uriel.

"Quite," Morgan said, smiling.

"I'm gay, in case you couldn't tell." Uriel chuckled as he pretended to brush long hair back behind his ear.

"Aren't we all?" Trevor quipped, announcing his arrival. "Hello, my love," he said, planting a kiss on Uriel's forehead.

"No funny business, ladies. He's all mine." Uriel beamed as he looked up at Trevor.

Uriel and Trevor also lived in Morgan's building, down the hall from Victor. They owned and operated Glass Half Full—an eco-friendly bath and body store where green was the name of the game and in-house production and customization set them apart. You want lemon to be the scent of all your household cleaners and personal items? You got it. Bring in your own containers or return the ones already purchased from the store, and they would thank you on their social media as the "Environmental Impact Warrior" of the day. You would get a badge and everything.

"Back to what I was saying," Uriel stated, rolling his eyes. "I swear, someone let the squirrel out of its cage one too many times today. I can't keep this train of thought on the tracks. Now, what is it we were talking about? Oh, yes. She has to do something, 'O' says. Tell us dear 'O'?" Uriel pointed to Olivia. "What does this lovely little nymph need to do?"

"I was just saying that she needs to hook up with a girl. At least once."

"I'm not sure what all the fuss is about?" Uriel said, scrunching his nose.

"Never tried it, huh?" Morgan asked, her eyes fixed on Uriel.

"Hard pass." He scowled. "Don't get me wrong, I love women. Women are beautiful. And occasionally, if you are privileged enough to witness it, I play one." He chuckled.

"You're a drag queen?" Morgan squealed, bouncing up and down in her seat like an excited child.

"'The' drag queen, honey. Miss Nöe Stalgia. Yes, yes. I know. It is an honor and a privilege to be in the presence of one such as myself. Contain your enthusiasm, please." Uriel pretended to hide his face from the paparazzi, shooing the invisible intruder away with his other hand.

"You'll have to invite me to a show sometime. I've never been, and I must experience it," Morgan said excitedly.

"You must and you shall, honey. Next show you can sit in the front row. Hell, I'll do you one better; I will honor you with backstage access. You can thank me later." Uriel shook his hand dismissively toward Morgan.

"Thank you!" Morgan exclaimed.

"I said later, bitch," Uriel teased, deepening his voice as his head shot back toward Morgan and he scowled.

The group finished their drinks and ended their afternoon with a walk back to the lofts. Olivia joined them, but had her Uber pick her up just outside. "Well..." Olivia said as a crossover vehicle pulled up, "this is me."

Before she opened the door to get in, the front door of Morgan's building opened and out strode the "Trust Fund Baby" himself. He looked in their direction, smirked as he shook his head, and jogged across the street to his vehicle, where he jumped in and quickly drove away.

"What was that?" Olivia asked as her eyes widened, a grin creeping across her face.

"Nothing to worry your pretty little head about, 'O'," Morgan insisted.

"It wasn't my head that was doing the thinking. Girl, that man is fine with a capital 'F.' As in, I'm going to fuck the shit right out of him."

"That would be more Uriel and I's area of expertise, wouldn't you say?" Trevor joked.

"You did not just go there? Honey! You see, girls? Can't take this man anywhere. He's insatiable, I tell you." Uriel sighed.

"Absolutely ravenous," Trevor said as he bit Uriel's earlobe. "How about we skip the small talk and head upstairs for a nightcap?"

"You had me at head. Sorry, girls. You're on your own. I've matters to attend to... and by matters, I mean-"

"We get it," Olivia interrupted. "Get out of here, you crazy kids."

Once the door closed and Uriel and Trevor were in the elevator on their way upstairs, Olivia asked Morgan again, "Now what's the deal with tall, dark, and fuck me now?"

"No deal. There was just a moment this one time."

"And by moment you mean?" Olivia trailed off.

"By moment, I mean that Jamison Masters is a self-absorbed, egotistical, rich kid with little to offer in terms of conversation."

"Who said anything about conversation?" Olivia smirked.

"Gross, 'O'. Look, if there is anything I have loads of experience in identifying, it's assholes. And that guy is the blueprint they all originated from. Sure, he's hot, but he is a grade 'A' piece. And by 'A', I mean asshole with a capital 'A'."

CHAPTER 3

GIRLS' NIGHT OUT

"You are going to be ready to go sometime tonight, right?" Olivia asked as she stood impatiently in Morgan's bedroom later that night.

"Yes 'O'. But you of all people should know that you can't rush perfection. And this..." Morgan said as she pulled open her robe to display the lingerie she had on underneath. "Well, this, Bitch, is a work of art," she said as she shook her ass in Olivia's direction.

"The vibes I am getting are less Leonardo DaVinci and more Moulin Rouge, that's for sure. Where the hell did you get that?" Nora exaggerated as she stood appraising the lace ensemble Morgan was wearing.

Morgan swiped vanilla flavored body powder across her cleavage as she smiled over at Nora. "It's one of the perks," Morgan announced as she turned back to the mirror, pursing her red lips and checking her teeth before blowing herself a kiss.

"One perk of what?" Olivia chimed in.

"Didn't I tell you? I got a new side hustle." Morgan giggled.

"What kind of side hustle has... how much was this thing?"

Olivia questioned as she ran her fingers along the lace detailing and satiny straps that crisscrossed their way across Morgan's breasts.

"To answer your question..." Morgan smirked, "a lot. The side hustle, my dear Olivia, is compliments of Allison."

"Allison?" Nora asked. "Like, catering Allison?"

"The same. You know Allison's a design student, right? At the University?"

"Yeah."

"Well..." Morgan continued, "Allison just so happens to intern over at SSC Intimates."

"Isn't that like a kink brand?" Olivia interrupted.

"Yes," Morgan said, drawing out her reply. "Among other things. And I know what you're thinking, but not everything is whips and chains, and 'Oh, Daddy, please spank me'." Morgan moaned.

"Wait? Is that thing crotchless?" Nora gasped. She snapped the straps that fastened at Morgan's hips. "You do plan on wearing something over it, right?"

"Do I have to?" Morgan pouted. "It's just so pretty," she said, admiring herself as she ran her hands up along her collarbone, tracing her thumb across her lip before biting it.

Nora's eyes just widened, and Morgan couldn't help but laugh.

"Relax, Nor. I'll put something over it. I would hate to offend your delicate sensibilities," she teased in her most convincing southern belle accent.

"How much have you already had to drink?" Olivia questioned as Morgan raised her wine glass once again to her lips.

She finished the glass and lowered it. "Not enough. Come on. Help me pick something out if Nora insists I cover up."

Morgan motioned toward her closet.

"I see somebody's planning to get laid tonight," Olivia sang.

"If I have my way, there will be strap marks across my ass and this little number will be soaking wet beside the bed come morning," Morgan said as she ran her fingers across a dress in her closet.

Nora just shook her head and walked out of the bedroom, as Olivia and Morgan dug through the closet to find something appropriate to ensure that Morgan succeeded in her task for the evening.

Olivia Andrews and Nora Walters worked with Morgan at the hotel, where she took over the concierge position. The hotel wasn't part of a chain, but the company who owned it also owned the property she'd worked at in Minnesota. She accepted the position when she applied for an inter-company transfer to get her out of Minneapolis and away from all the uncomfortable memories that city now represented. A way for her to escape everything that would bring her thoughts back to Eric, the fiasco that was their engagement party, and ultimately the end of their five-year relationship; crashing and burning as she turned the corner to witness Eric making out with Emma, one of his sister's friends.

Morgan had changed a lot since that night. She left everything and everyone she knew and ended up in this foreign place. Somewhere she could start over with a clean slate and no longer be seen just as the fiancée of Eric Watkins, of the prominent Minneapolis Watkins'. She stepped into a role she was unprepared for in a city that was not her own, but knew she had to make the best of it, because there was no going back to Minnesota.

It is hard being a concierge in a city you know nothing about, and in a place where you have no connections. Sure, the last concierge had her "book of wonders," containing the names and phone numbers of all the go to florists, and the contact information of every maître d and restauranteur in the city. But having their number doesn't give you a seat at their table or the ability to reach out for favors. Morgan couldn't just call up the theatre for tickets or get that must have table at the hottest restaurant, because no one knew her. She was a nobody and fulfilling the responsibilities of a concierge with no connections was going to be hard.

Morgan wasted no time introducing herself to every bar tender and hostess downtown, starting with Olivia, the manager at the lounge in her hotel.

One night out with Olivia and Morgan was well on her way. They would meet up for drinks after work and partake in rounds of golf at the club on the weekend, hoping to find just that one person whose friendship would solidify Morgan's importance and be the "in" she needed to succeed.

Morgan started attending every wine tasting, offered her tastebuds to sample the newest dish at every restaurant, and, if the people she was required to rub elbows with just so happened to be male, she would go all out with the charm, ending the inter-action with a hint of innuendo. It's amazing how many doors opened and how many opportunities presented themselves to her when men thought a young, beautiful woman might be interested in them. And tonight, with Olivia and Nora at her side, it would be a trio of young, beautiful women. The men at the bar didn't stand a chance.

Walking out of the stairwell, Olivia looked over at her friends and asked, "So, what's your poison? Will it be Envy, Minx, or Voodoo?"

"None of the above, honey," Uriel interrupted as he and Trevor stepped out of the elevator and into the lobby where the girls now stood. "You bitches look too good to waste your time at those places with all those frat bros. There would be no escaping the wandering hands and their off-tempo grinding all up on your ass."

"I don't know, Uriel. All that sounds fine to me." Morgan smirked.

"Girl? Know your worth, and oh my god… what in Persephone's temptation palace are you wearing?" Uriel gasped.

"It's crotchless," Nora informed him.

"It's positively sinful. And honey… I love it!" Uriel beamed.

"Uber for five?" Trevor asked.

"Any chance you'd be willing to make that six?" Victor inquired as he stepped out of the stairwell and into the foyer behind Morgan and her friends.

"I don't see why not?" Olivia smiled as Morgan elbowed her in the side. "What? It's like you said, he's harmless." She leaned in and whispered to Morgan, "Besides, if you're lucky, the resident asshole will make an appearance as well."

"Bite your fucking tongue, 'O'. Don't wish that evil on me or I will go right back upstairs and call it a night."

Victor had been eavesdropping and chimed in with, "Well, if you decide to stay in, I have a great movie we can watch. Order in some pizza, toss back a couple, and just relax a bit? It could be fun."

"Sorry to rain on your parade," Nora spoke up, looking straight at Victor. "But the only thing Morgan plans on tossing back tonight is her legs in the air."

"Nora!" Olivia squealed. "Well done, bitch. I didn't think you had it in you."

"And if things go my way," Morgan said, looking at Uriel and Trevor. "My new bestie Uriel over here will find me someone to put something in me."

Victor looked uncomfortable at all the innuendo, and cringed when Morgan announced her plans for the evening. He was not one to look at or speak to women in that manner, and despite how attractive he found Morgan, her brazenness took him aback.

Victor didn't get it because Morgan looked so clean cut and wholesome. So girl next door. Sure, her skin was flawless and always seemed to glisten, and when she stood close to him, her scent was intoxicating. But the way she talked, the way she was so open about her body, and the way she verbalized what she wanted done to her. It just wasn't right and he couldn't stomach it.

"Why do you do that?" Victor questioned Morgan as they waited.

"Why do I do what?"

"Why is everything you say about getting laid and having sex? Don't you respect yourself more than that?"

"Are you being serious with me right now?" Morgan asked with her mouth agape. She pulled a mini bottle of fireball from her purse and downed it as he looked on. "Look, Victor. I'm sure that you are an absolute gentleman. And one day you will make some clean cut, cookie cutter, bred to be a housewife girl, the happiest woman in the world. But that is not me."

"Ain't that the fucking truth," Jamison announced as he stepped out of the stairwell behind them, stopping with the door ajar.

"Oh, I'm sorry. I didn't realize we invited you to take part in this conversation?" Morgan scowled at Jamison as he stood there, leaning against the doorjamb.

"It's a public place. And even though no one invited me, I felt it was my duty to save this, what looks to be a good upstanding citizen..." Jamison motioned toward Victor, "from the likes of a succubus like you."

"That's an awful big word for someone with that much gel in his hair," Morgan sneered.

"You two are absolutely adorable," Uriel teased. "When's the wedding?"

Stifled laughter filled the foyer as Morgan's friends choked.

"I thought we were friends, Uriel. You take that threat out of your mouth this instant." Morgan winced.

"You could be so lucky." Jamison laughed, letting the door close behind him with a snick before stepping past the girls. "I wouldn't pay to fuck you." Jamison tossed the insult in Morgan's face and then walked out the door.

Jogging across the street, Jamison climbed into the passenger side of a Denali with blue under glow, as the bass from the speakers shook the glass doors of the entryway.

"See? I told you he was a fucking asshole," Morgan announced.

⌐LIVE•¬

"Grey Goose Martini, extra-dirty, two olives," Morgan yelled out when the bartender motioned toward her.

"You aren't fucking around?" Nora laughed.

"Look, I haven't had a night out that wasn't tied to work and making connections since I got here," Morgan said, throwing a twenty on the bar as she winked at the bartender before turning and walking away with Nora. "I'm not about to waste this opportunity to get laid." She chuckled before running into the back of someone, spilling her drink all down the front of her dress. "Fuck!"

"Yes, please... but also, my bad," the man said who's back she had run into as he turned around to face her.

"It's fine." She huffed. "It's my fucking fault for not paying attention to where I was going," she shouted over the music.

"At least let me buy you another?"

"If you insist." Morgan smiled, her eyes widening as she turned toward Nora.

"After you?" The man motioned toward the bar, following behind her.

As Morgan and her stranger stepped up to the bar, the same server turned to face her. "Back again so soon?" the bartender teased.

"It appears my grip isn't what it used to be," Morgan flirted, leaning on the bar with her ass in the air as the bartender went to remaking her order.

"Oh, I doubt that," the bartender flirted back, licking his lips when as he pushed her drink in front of her.

Morgan lowered herself from the bar, and then she and her mystery man turned back into the crowd. They milled through slowly, stopping several paces from the bar.

"As do I," the mystery man whispered in Morgan's ear as he pressed himself up against her. "Sorry about that. It's crowded here. How about we take our drinks and find some place with more room, and maybe a little quieter so we can talk and get to know each other better? I'm Lucas, by the way."

That was Morgan's fifth time at the bar that night and she was past the point of tipsy, so this mystery man presented the opportunity she had been waiting the entire night for.

She pressed her ass back into Lucas and arched her back. "Morgan," she moaned. "Talking's overrated. But you give me some more room to maneuver and I'll take you up on your offer to get to know you better," she said, grabbing his hand and placing it along the hem of her skirt.

Lucas accepted the invitation and ran his fingertips along the inside of her thigh, just beneath the edge of her skirt. "Your skin is so fucking soft," he sighed in her ear.

"I exfoliate." Morgan laughed, nothing but mischief in her eyes as she was being pulled away by Nora.

"Duty calls," Nora said, looking back at Lucas. "Sorry, guy. We go to the bathroom in twos."

Morgan turned her head and winked at Lucas as Nora pulled her through the crowd. "Until next time..." her voice trailed off as the music drowned out the rest of what she said.

"What?" he yelled after her.

Morgan blew Lucas a kiss and then turned, taking a sip from her glass as she passed by the bar on her way to the bathroom.

"Hey!" the bartender called out.

"Yeah?" Morgan giggled as she stumbled and stopped, forcing Nora to stop as well.

Nora looked on in agitation as Morgan flirted with yet another guy.

"That dude opened a tab for you," the bartender offered.

"What?" Morgan squealed.

"Said you can have whatever you want!"

"Whatever I want?" Morgan asked as she ran her tongue along the rim of her martini glass.

"That you can have for free," the bartender flirted. "I get off at two."

"Oh, she'll get off well before then," Nora interrupted as she continued to pull Morgan toward the restrooms.

"I wasn't finished!" Morgan pouted. "And he was hot as fuck."

"Yes, and is just as interested in fucking you as he is in the dude that bought your drink."

"Shut up?" Morgan exaggerated.

"You are aware this is a gay bar, right?"

"No, it's not," Morgan slurred.

"Yes, honey, it is. The Garden, as in, the place of original sin?" Nora explained.

"That's not why they named it that."

"Well, maybe not, but that doesn't change the fact that this is, in fact, a gay bar."

"Gay bar or not, you've got to ease up on all the cock-blocking you're doing tonight." Morgan scowled.

"I'm not blocking anything!" Nora exclaimed.

"If you want to fuck me, just say so." Morgan sighed before pulling Nora's mouth to hers, planting a sloppy wet kiss on her mouth.

Just then, Olivia walked up to where Nora and Morgan stood in line for the restroom and called out, "I said to hook up with a woman. I didn't mean right away. And I never intended for it to be with Nora!"

"This evening just got more interesting!" Uriel hissed, stopping in his tracks after exiting the restroom. "Welcome to the Garden, ladies and gentlemen," he announced as he threw his hands in the air, causing some girls in the hallway to whistle. "Now, hurry your asses up and get out there and join us. There's business to attend to."

Once out of the restroom, Olivia drug Morgan behind her as she followed Uriel and Nora to the dance floor. Trevor, being the chill guy that he is, just stood at the edge of the crowd watching as all his friends gyrated, rubbing all over one another as the alcohol and music kicked their party into high gear.

No one existed outside their circle. They paid no mind to any of the slick bodies that were dancing just outside of their bubble, or to any of the people that tried to disrupt their groove.

Morgan and Olivia closed their eyes, letting their bodies move to the music as their hands wandered and they ground up on one another. Every touch of Olivia's hands, and every caress of Nora's fingertips, sent Morgan's head spinning as the ecstasy kicked in.

"What did you take?" Olivia asked as she breathed into Morgan's neck.

"Judging by the rate of your breathing and the way your eyes keep rolling into the back of your head; same as you." Morgan grinned.

"We have to work tomorrow!" Olivia sighed.

"It will be rough, that's for sure."

"Fuck it," Olivia said.

"I'm hoping so," Morgan shouted, as she stared over to where an unidentified hot piece of ass was chatting up Trevor as they stood watching them all. "Who's that?"

"Kent, something or another!" Olivia called out, nowhere near quietly.

Kent must have heard his name because he perked up and looked over, making eye contact with Morgan.

"Why? Do you like?" Olivia smiled.

"Oh, I like." Morgan grinned as Olivia trailed her fingertips down her collarbone.

"Would you like him to come over?"

"Yes, please."

Olivia forced Morgan's head to the side, tilting it away from her with her nose before trailing her tongue down the line of Morgan's neck. As she looked to where Kent stood, she made sure they had his attention. She wrapped her arms around Morgan and pulled her body back into hers as she grated her teeth across her collarbone.

"O." Morgan moaned out as the sensation took over.

"That's a girl. That did it. Here he comes," Olivia announced as Kent walked through the crowd toward them.

Kent stopped just in front of the two women, who swayed back and forth as they melted into one another, giggling to themselves.

"You two are having way too much fun over here by your lone-some," Kent stated.

"I'm not lonesome," Olivia flirted. "I'm occupied," she said, running her hand up Morgan's dress and pinching her nipple through the fabric, causing her to moan out. She didn't break eye contact with Kent, not even for a second.

"Do you mind if I give you a hand?" Kent asked, looking at Olivia and then down at Morgan as she stood in front of him, leaning back against Olivia.

"Be my guest," Olivia offered. "Morgan?" Olivia sought permission.

"The more the merrier." Morgan grinned as she looked into Kent's eyes.

Kent was a dark-haired, deep blue-eyed, sculpted piece of absolute chiseled perfection. Every inch of him looked like pure rippling muscle, including his facial features. He had deep-set eyes, a strong jawline, protruding chin, and a sloped nose that, if she had to guess, he'd looked down on many a woman that had crossed his path. Morgan wondered if he would normally consider her beneath him, or if the possibility of getting her freak in between the sheets was enough for him to lower his standards, just this once.

He's a finance bro. He has to be. Everything about this man screams out, "Let's talk about how to diversify your portfolio!"

"Morgan, was it?" Kent asked as he ran his fingers up her arm.

"Uh, huh." She sighed as she closed her eyes and gave in to the sensations as they overwhelmed her.

"As shocking as this may come to you," he said as he leaned in closer. "I'm not in the habit of putting my hands in places they might otherwise not be welcome. Do you understand?"

"Huh, uh?" Morgan motioned her head from side to side as her grin widened.

"As tempting as this opportunity, and you are," he whispered in her ear, brushing his lips along the lower edge of her earlobe. "I'd rather wait until I can have you begging for it. Why take something when you can earn it?"

"Earnings, dividends, stock options." She giggled.

"Okay? Now you've lost me."

"I was just trying to turn you on by speaking your language," she cooed as she inched her hands up his chest, running them underneath the fabric of his button up dress shirt. "Do we meet later to talk futures?" she teased.

"I stick to the legal side of business. I'll pass on the finance mumbo jumbo," he said, grabbing her by the wrists and stopping her as her hands wandered.

"Potato. Potato," she slurred.

"Alright, sleeping beauty," he laughed, brushing a gentle kiss on her forehead. "We'll continue this conversation at another time." Kent motioned to Olivia. "I think your friend is ready to go," he said as he held Morgan up and she swayed back and forth.

"Oh, I'm ready to go." Morgan sighed, running her hands down her dress, and lifting the edge of her skirt as she traced her index finger across her lips before raising it to her mouth where she sucked it clean right in his face.

"Okay!" exclaimed Nora as she looked at Morgan and Olivia disapprovingly. "Time to go. Trevor!" Nora called out. "A little help?"

"Nora," Morgan groaned. "I thought we were friends?"

"We are friends," Nora answered in exasperation. "But you are way too out of it to make certain decisions at the moment."

Looking up at Nora as she escorted her out of The Garden, Morgan once again made her sentiments known. "Cock blocker," she accused as Nora ushered her to wait for their Uber.

"I've been called worse," Nora admitted, holding Morgan up as they waited just outside the bar.

Their car pulled up, and Nora opened the door. "Now get your ass in, you lush. Olivia!" Nora yelled out. "Get the fuck in the car!"

Olivia stood at the door of the club, chatting with Kent as Trevor exited. "Wait! Can you go close her tab?" Olivia called out to Trevor, grabbing his arm.

Trevor walked back inside and waved down the bartender. "I need to close out a tab."

"What's the name?" he asked.

"Morgan Ericksson."

The bartender shuffled through the cards and then came back to Trevor. "I have no Morgan Ericksson."

"It was the girl in the black sequin dress and gold heels," Trevor announced.

"Oh, yeah," the bartender said as he realized who they were talking about. "I don't have a card on file for that one."

"Here," Trevor said as he scribbled Morgan's number onto a napkin and handed it to the bartender. "Call and leave her a message and she'll come settle up tomorrow."

"That's unnecessary," Lucas said as he grabbed the napkin away from the bartender, placing it in his pocket. "I'm taking care of it, remember?"

"I completely forgot," the bartender said, making eyes at Lucas.

"Sure you did," Lucas said as he took another sip of his drink and looked over as Trevor waited for Uriel to join him. "See she gets home safe?"

Trevor nodded before walking away as Uriel followed right behind him.

As they walked out the door, Uriel asked Trevor, "What was that?"

"I'll tell you in the car," Trevor assured him, kissing his cheek as he wrapped his arm around his back.

Lucas watched from the bar as Trevor and Uriel stepped through the front door. He turned back to his drink on the bar top.

"See who gets home safe?" Jamison asked, teasing Lucas as he stepped up behind him, squeezing and shaking his shoulders.

"Eavesdrop much? Just the fucking hottest chick I've seen in a long time," Lucas boasted, holding up the napkin he'd slipped into his pocket earlier.

"What's that?" asked Kent as he walked up next to Jamison and Lucas.

"Hey, fucker?" Jamison punched Kent in the shoulder.

"Not that fucking arm, man. You know better," Kent said.

"Right. Ricky Fowler over here has plans for the PGA," Jamison teased.

"Fuck off, dude. I'm good, but I'm not that good." Kent rubbed his arm.

"If you ask me, you are working too hard," Lucas said as he finished his drink.

"Not all of us have mommy or daddy's money, assholes," Kent reminded them.

"Dude, you're gonna be a fucking lawyer. Money's money, whether earned or in a trust." Jamison sneered.

"Says the guy who hasn't had to work a day in his life. Between you and the Arabian Prince over here," Kent poked.

"Fuck off, man. I'm a U.S. citizen," Lucas said, pushing Kent. "And to answer your question, it's just the number of my Arabian Princess."

"You're not getting married. Probably ever," Jamison joked.

"Fine. Then it's the number of the girl I can't wait to fuck," Lucas countered.

"That sounds more like it," Kent said. "What about you, Jamison? Get any action lined up tonight?"

"I'll leave the bar flies to you two. I prefer my women with a little more varied tastes," Jamison admitted.

"How could I forget?" Lucas grinned. "Sticks and stones and all that."

"Yeah." Kent snorted. "But whips and chains are just the beginning with this sick fuck."

"There is nothing wrong with my sex life. I am beyond satisfied," Jamison boasted.

"When was the last time you hooked up with anyone, anyway?" Lucas asked.

"Quality over quantity, dick heads. One day you'll get it, and until then..." Jamison said, motioning toward their hands, "make sure you keep lotion on those to keep them smooth, because they are the only action you're gonna get."

"You're an asshole with a capital 'A', you know that?" Kent asserted.

"So I've been told."

CHAPTER 4

HINDSIGHT

Olivia held Morgan's face under the water in the ice-filled sink. "Keep your face submerged!"

Morgan came up gasping, spitting water as she struggled to inhale. "I can't fucking breathe, hoe!"

"I'm the hoe?" Olivia shrieked, laughing aloud. "I'm not the one who got fingered in every corner of the bar last night, am I?"

Olivia had a valid point, but she didn't get fingered, not one time—other than by herself. And even if Olivia had a point, that didn't make her any less of a hoe. She displayed hoe tendencies, so the pot shouldn't be calling the kettle black.

"What does that have to do with the price of tea in China?" Morgan scoffed.

"My God. You are so old. Who the fuck even says stuff like that?" Olivia teased.

"My mom used to say it all the time."

"Precisely," Olivia pointed out. "Now, head back in the water."

"Why am I doing this again?"

"I saw it on a video. It's supposed to be an immediate hang-

❦ 33 ❦

over cure. Now, deep breath and back under you go," Olivia insisted, grabbing Morgan by the back of her neck and forcing her face back in the sink.

It was seven thirty in the morning on Friday, and Olivia and Morgan were due to work at 9 a.m. Their window of opportunity to come out of their haze from the alcohol and the other party favors they partook in the night prior was dwindling, so they had better get a move on.

Most of the previous evening was a blur, and the last face Morgan recalled seeing, before it all went dark, was that of the asshole in her building who intentionally closed the door on her several weeks back, watching from the doorway as Nora escorted her out of the club. Of all the people she could have run into on a night when she was primed for action and in the mood to scratch her itch. *Why him?* The fates must've been fucking with her, because he was the last person on earth she'd ever fuck.

As Morgan stood in the bathroom, wringing the water out of her hair, her phone rang obnoxiously loud. "Make it fucking stop!" she yelled.

"Relax," Olivia called out. "I've got it. Just keep getting ready."

"Morgan Ericksson's phone. Head bitch speaking." Olivia chuckled.

"What? No, you're fucking not. I am," Melissa argued.

"Morgan!" Olivia shouted over the sound of the hair dryer. "It's Melissa!"

"Tell her I'll have to call her back," she called out.

"She says she'll have to-"

"Yeah, yeah. I heard her," Melissa groaned as she interrupted Olivia. "Tell her not to fucking forget like last time."

Olivia covered the phone with her palm and called out, "She says you better not forget, like last time."

"Bitch! I won't fucking forget," Morgan said, stomping across the room and taking the phone from Olivia. "I won't forget, okay! I have to go or I'm going to be late!"

"Fine," Melissa pouted.

"You fine!" Morgan shouted. She lowered her voice and continued, "Seriously, Melissa. I won't forget. But I have to call you back later."

"Love you."

"Love you more," Morgan replied as she hung up the phone.

"Here." Olivia thrust a glass of orange juice into Morgan's face as she buttoned the cuffs of her blouse.

"I can't drink that. I just brushed my teeth."

"Trust me, you need it. And once you have one taste of it, you're going to want it," Olivia explained.

"It's just orange juice. I've never been a huge fan-"

"Just fucking drink it!" Olivia huffed.

"Okay. Okay. Damn. What's got your panties in a bunch this morning?"

"Oh, I don't know, maybe the after-ecstasy death feeling that I have going on. Everything hurts: my teeth, my jaw, and my back. I am fucking miserable."

"Don't blame me for the way you feel right now. I'm not the one who gave it to you. I may not feel as shitty as you do, but I still feel like ass."

"Which I don't fucking get because you had way more to drink than me, and then you took a pill. So, how in the hell are you even able to function right now?"

"I don't know. Just fucking lucky, I guess."

"Well, it's not fucking fair. I have a large order coming in today and no extra help to get it put away. So, I'm on my own," Olivia complained.

"Relax. Have Seth help you get it all put away. He doesn't have to do anything with the bar until later this evening. And if you still need help, run over and grab Quentin. Supposedly, they hired another bell boy, so there should be plenty of idle hands to assist you."

"There had better be because I feel terrible. And I don't have the patience nor the energy to get this all done today by myself."

"Fear not, dear 'O'. I'll see to it personally."

⌈LIVE•⌋

Olivia and Morgan arrived at the hotel just ten minutes shy of 9:00 a.m. After they clocked in, Morgan turned around and ran straight into Jamison Masters.

"What the fuck is he doing here?" she asked Quentin.

"He's the new bellhop."

"Since when?"

"Since today. I thought the orientation packet made it obvious?" Jamison said matter-of-factly, lifting his folder.

"Nobody asked you." Morgan scowled.

"Didn't your mother ever tell you it's not nice to make faces at people? If you hold it too long, it might stay that way."

"Oh, I'm certain as long as you're around, it's going to stay that way."

"Good. You're all here," Alexander said. "Allow me to introduce Mr. Masters. He is filling the bell staff position as of today. Be nice and show him the ropes, won't you?"

"Oh, I'll show him the ropes, alright," Morgan said through gritted teeth as she fake smiled for the General Manager. Whispering to Olivia, she continued, "I can't guarantee he'll like what I do with the ropes once I've shown them to him. But that's a problem for another time."

Jamison walked over and leaned in so only Olivia and Morgan

could hear and said, "Ropes are kind of my specialty. So, bring it on, little girl. There's little you could do that would phase me." He straightened his jacket, adjusted his tie, and then smiled at Olivia. Jamison then turned and followed Quentin out of the break room.

"Did you fucking hear that, asshole?" Morgan scoffed.

"Yeah. But did you?" Olivia questioned Morgan as she raised her eyebrows.

"Oh, I fucking heard him. I don't believe him one bit. But I heard him."

Morgan spent most of that day in her office. She checked in on Olivia several times to see if she needed any help with her delivery, but each time she stepped into the lounge, the asshole was there.

Jamison had the suit jacket of his uniform off and, much to Morgan's dismay, that put his fitted button up dress shirt tucked into his tight slacks on display. It took everything in her power to not walk over and smack his robust ass. But seeing as she didn't want to have a visit with HR soon, and for several other reasons, she refrained.

No, no, no. You will not be thinking about those things regarding this asshole!

Later that evening, once the lounge was well into happy hour and the bar was about to open its doors for the five o'clock regulars, Morgan got a moment with Olivia. "Well, how was it?" Morgan asked.

"How was what?" Olivia looked at her sideways.

"Being forced to spend the day with 'Mr. Masters'?" Morgan exaggerated as she made air quotes with her fingers.

"It wasn't terrible. For starters, he was helpful. And he's not that bad. Another thing, he smells fucking amazing." She swooned.

"Olivia, no!" Morgan pouted. "You're not supposed to like this dude."

"I'm sorry," Olivia pleaded. "I didn't get the memo."

"That's bullshit and you know it. You knew I loathed him, and you still made goo-goo eyes. Gross. I thought you had better taste than that?"

"My taste is just fine. And like I said, he's not that bad." Olivia lifted her shoulders.

"Let's just agree to disagree," Morgan said as she crossed her arms in agitation.

"Then disagree we shall, because I'm about to meet him in the bar for a drink. You are more than welcome to give him a second chance and join us?"

"Nope. I'm going to go upstairs, check on catering, and see if they need any help. Because, apparently, you have lost your mind."

"Morgan? Don't be like that," Olivia called out after her as she walked away. "Morgan!"

"You about ready for that drink?" Jamison asked, walking up behind Olivia with his eyes on the stairwell Morgan just disappeared into.

"Let's do it." Olivia beamed as she walked beside Jamison into the bar, taking a seat in front of Seth as Jamison ordered them each a round.

I can't believe that little traitor! The nerve of that girl. All that time devoted to getting to know her and she just ups and ditches me for some dude! This is the beginning of the end of us. I just know it, Morgan thought as she stomped up the stairs.

Morgan pulled her phone out of her pocket, put her earbuds in, and called Siri to action. "Hey Siri?"

"Yes."

"Call Melissa Watkins, mobile."

"Calling Melissa Watkins, mobile," Siri chimed back.

One ring. Two. Three. *Hey, this is Melissa. If I don't answer, it should have been a text, bitch!*

"I can't believe she sent me to voicemail," Morgan said, offended.

Morgan made her way into the catering pantry and was helping to fold and put away linens when Allison walked in, smiling from ear to ear. They stood, sharing silent smirks and grins with one another as they worked, and as Morgan continued to fold, she remembered her encounter with Allison the week before.

Morgan had been doing that day, just as she was now, folding and putting away linens in the catering pantry, when Allison walked in and pulled her from her thoughts.

"Someone is having a good evening. What's with all the teeth?" Morgan asked.

Allison walked up to Morgan and started whispering. "So you know I'm an art student, right? Well, a fashion design student, actually. But an art student?"

"Yeah?"

"I have been interning at this 'apparel' company," Allison said, making air quotes. "Anyway. The owner was talking earlier today with her advertising and marketing people, and had said something about looking for fresh faces for her brand, to get ready for her European launch."

"And her advertising campaign has you smiling this brightly because, why?"

"Because she asked me, 'If it was my brand, what I would do?' She asked me how I would select my models and narrow down who would be the face of the brand for the next year."

"That's a good thing, right? Her valuing your opinion enough to ask?"

"It's a phenomenal thing! And the best part about it is, she's going to use my idea!" Allison squealed.

"That's freaking amazing. So, are you going to leave me hanging, or are you going to tell me what this amazing idea was?"

"Okay. Imagine you are an up-and-coming brand and you want to get your name out there. What's the best way to do that right now?"

"What is it somebody told me? It's not about what you know, it's about who you know."

"Exactly. So, I told her I would use social media to select the next face and ambassador for my brand. And that's what she's going to do! She's opening applications for people to become brand ambassadors and compete to have a chance of becoming the face of her next campaign."

"So, when do all these shenanigans start?" Morgan inquired.

Allison pulled out her phone and opened her social media. She scrolled twice and then turned the screen around to Morgan. "The clock is ticking. And the countdown ends in 72 hours."

"That is not a hell of a lot of time to find a face for a brand. Why the rush?"

"Once she selects the different candidates, she will schedule them all for test shoots and fittings. They'll compile the photographs and information about the applicants and make the final decision. But they don't have a lot of time because the photo shoot for the catalogue and all the advertising for the European launch is only a couple of weeks out."

"Allison, you don't know how much I want to kiss you right now. I have been racking my brain for weeks trying to figure out another side hustle to keep me occupied and make me a little more money while I'm here in town. I don't know how long they intend to keep me as the concierge, and I'm not even sure if this is what I want to do long term. So, I like to keep my options open," Morgan admitted.

"I appreciate your enthusiasm, Morgan. But I think before you apply I should tell you something."

"What?"

"The lady I intern for is Alessandra Escobedo. Her brand is SSC Intimates."

"Okay. Well, I haven't heard of it. But modeling is modeling," Morgan shrugged.

"You're not wrong, Morgan. I'm just saying her brand is some-what niche."

"And by niche, you mean?"

"By niche, I mean it's a lifestyle brand. SSC intimates is a kink and fetish brand. You know, intimate apparel and playthings."

"So. What's the problem?" Morgan placed her hands on her hips.

"No problem. I just didn't think that would be something you would be into," Allison admitted.

"My dear Allison," Morgan chuckled, stepping into her. "I won't hold it against you. Because, after all, you don't know what you don't know." Morgan winked before walking away. "Send me that link," she called back down the hall.

The memory of that night continued with Morgan pulling out all her photography equipment and setting up several backdrops in her living area. She did some light research into Alessandra and the brand, and looked at what other designers in the industry were doing for their marketing and advertising.

Once she had selected what she deemed appropriate outfits for the submission, she did her hair and makeup, and got into character. A couple glasses of wine and she was ready.

Morgan fastened her mask behind her head and then reap-plied her lipstick before she posed herself on her chaise lounge.

With her phone positioned in the center of her ring light, she pressed down on the remote control in her hand and streamed.

"Come out, come out wherever you are. Who's ready to play?" she asked seductively as she looked into the camera while sucking on a lollipop. She circled her tongue slowly around the end. "Well, if it isn't you again?" she said, looking into the camera. "Scrooge McDuck, was it? At least that is the image you have chosen for your profile. Careful now. You're aging yourself, Mr. McDuck," she teased, her sultry giggle filling the room.

"Now, where were we? Oh, yes... you were just about to tell me all the things you wanted to do to me. But first, I must ask a question: Did you miss me?"

Morgan blacked out her screen, and immediately, Mr. Moneybags paid tribute. "You can do better than that, Unka Scrooge," she laughed. "That's it. That's more like it." Once she reached the goal she had set, she turned her camera back on and continued with their rendezvous. "Oh, how I enjoy our playtime together. What game should we play tonight?"

Morgan finished her live stream, and the follow-on session with Mr. Moneybags, fastening her robe at her waist before she started drafting her submission for the SSC Intimates brand ambassador search.

A couple of still photos and a short clip introducing herself later, and Morgan was ready to hit the submit button, putting herself in the running to be the next face of the lifestyle brand.

This brand would be right up her alley, especially since she had been a natural when she first started streaming. The only difference was that she could openly show her face for the campaign, something she would not do for her online play sessions. Melissa didn't even know about her extracurricular activities and she planned to keep it that way.

CHAPTER 5
IT'S JUST COFFEE

"It's just coffee," Morgan defended herself as she Face Timed Melissa.

"If it's just coffee, then why the hell are we shaving our legs?"

Melissa always insisted on speaking in that manner. It was never just Morgan doing something or that he or she was doing something. It was always "we" were doing something. As in the royal sense. If there was ever a royal pain in Morgan's ass, it was Melissa.

"Did you ever think it was possible that I wanted to enjoy rubbing the smoothness of the length of my legs, and not that I was doing it for the benefit of someone else? Is that so far of a stretch?"

"Bitch, you can lie to yourself all you want, but I see that little smirk on your face. And I can hear your twat purring from here. She's all but crying out, 'Feed me, Morgan. I'm positively starv-ing,'" Melissa teased as she made little movements with her hands, her fingertips opening and closing as if they were a mouth.

"You're fucking ridiculous, you know that?" Morgan chastised her.

"Why are you getting mad at me? It's your pussy you should have a talking to. I'm just stating the obvious. The telltale signs are all there."

"How do you figure?"

"Well, let's see? We are shaving our legs, the bra and panty set we have on are matching, and I can see the teeth whitening tray on the counter behind us. We have checked all the boxes. So, yes, our pussy has an ulterior motive for today's 'coffee date'." Melissa exaggerated with air quotes.

"Yeah? Well, you're wrong. I pamper myself this way every day."

"Since fucking when? I have known you for five years and not once have I seen such a display except for... the day that shall not be named."

"Watch it," Morgan warned, scowling at Melissa through the video.

"I didn't say 'it' or talk about 'him'." Melissa shuddered. "He's fine, by the way. He's off finding himself in Costa Rica." Melissa rolled her eyes.

"Of course he is," Morgan scoffed. "Changing the subject: how was your cousin's wedding?"

"Oh, you mean the mating dance that was Miranda's nuptials? Waste of my damned time, if you ask me. So much puffery and preening. The peacocks were out in full force, and the hens? They were all fluffed up with nowhere to go."

"You sound jealous," Morgan teased.

"Bite your fucking tongue, bitch! Absolutely fucking not. I am one of the fortunate ones. I have zero interest in any of that stupidity."

"Not ever?" Morgan asked.

"Ever." Melissa shook her head as she moved her face ever so close to the camera. "Look into my eyes. Do you hear the words that are coming out of my mouth?" Melissa said in her most convincing Chris Rock impersonation. "Ever!"

"Duly noted," Morgan said as she dried off her legs and began lathering them up with her lotion.

"See!" Melissa screeched. "That too. That lotion." She pointed. "That lotion only appears on special occasions. If it's no big deal, then maybe you should tell your pussy that he isn't a special occasion."

"Stop! Enough, already. I get it. I never took enough care of myself in the past. So, now if I do, you think there is an ulterior motive. Rest assured, this is for me and me alone."

"And if he asks for a tour of Morgan's Gardens?"

"Remind me again why you named my lady bits Morgan's Gardens?" Morgan asked with one eyebrow raised in confusion.

"Oh, that's simple. Because everyone wants to take a walk in them."

⌜LIVE•⌟

Kent Granger Adams was in his early twenties and a collegiate golfer attending Drake University. He had grown up in Iowa City, where his mother, Evelyn, worked at the non-profit resource center as an administrative assistant. And his father, Grant, worked at Pleasant Valley Golf Course as the resident golf pro. That is where his love of golf was born and he developed his skill.

It was during those sessions with his father; he learned course management and fine-tuned his driving skills. He set the course record his junior year of high school in the driving championship, and that ensured bids for multiple scholarships from schools across the state.

He settled on Drake after his father set him up with one of his friends from college, who had a law office in Des Moines. It just made sense. Kent wanted to go into business law, so why not give him a leg up just in case his PGA hopes went unrealized?

"It's good to have a backup plan," his father had said. "You can stay at your home course as a pro all your life or you can ensure there are other options available to you if you change your mind."

Kent's father had given him sound advice and, for the first time, Kent took it.

"Grant and Evelyn beamed with joy on the day Kent signed with Drake," Morgan said aloud as she clicked from one press announcement to the next in Kent's name as she cyber stalked him.

Kent had messaged Morgan out of the blue one morning, a week after her night out, and invited her out for coffee after he got out of class later that afternoon. The number was unfamiliar, so she had to respond just to find out who it belonged to.

After he introduced himself and told the story about how they had met, because those details were rather fuzzy to her, he explained Olivia had given him her number as Nora was escorting her out of the club.

Morgan didn't agree to Kent's offer right away. She did some digging first, reaching out to the most obvious person to ask about him—Trevor.

Trevor filled her in with what little he knew, but his information wasn't useless. She learned his last name, and that opened an entire world of information once she started looking: articles about community service, pictures of matches he had won, and companies in Iowa City who had sponsored him for one tournament or another.

As far as optics were concerned, he appeared to be a well-rounded young man, and an all-around good-hearted individual. His story was one of, "small-town boy does good." There were worse narratives, that's for sure. So, she decided to see what all the hype was about.

Morgan had tried clean cut. That was what she thought Eric was, when he was anything but. Things were different now, at least for Morgan. She was no longer looking for a partner, or to settle down. Love was the furthest thing from her mind when chatting up the men she met. No, now was all about having fun. It was all about drinks to the wee hours and romps in the bar's backroom if her gentlemen callers were so inclined. She refused to be played for a fool anymore, and now she only wanted to play.

Okay. I will meet you for coffee. Where and when? I'll meet you there.

Smokey Row work for you? Say 3 p.m.?

See you then.

Can't wait.

"I'll show her Morgan's Gardens," Morgan said aloud as she walked into her closet, selecting a dark denim skirt and knee-high boots. "Mr. Adams will do far more than walk through Morgan's Gardens if this all goes well." She giggled, smiling at her reflection as she appraised herself with her skirt barely covering her ass cheeks. "Perfect," she called out, blowing a kiss to the mirror before grabbing her purse and keys as she headed toward the door.

Morgan stepped out of her apartment and was locking the door when a voice called out behind her.

"Where are we headed? And looking very nice, might I add," Victor announced.

"We… are not headed anywhere," Morgan replied dryly. "I am headed out to meet someone. No offense."

"None taken. I was just going to see if you wanted to do dinner sometime this week?"

"I can't. We have events all week, and I offered to help my catering staff," Morgan explained. "Maybe another time?"

"Can I hold you to that?"

Morgan turned around and faced Victor. "Look, Victor. You seem like a nice guy, but I'm just not interested in buying your brand at the moment."

"And what brand would that be?" Victor asked, stepping toward her.

"A nice guy," Morgan said, patting him on the shoulder. "I would chew you up and spit you out. And, to be honest… I wouldn't bat an eyelash. Sorry, man."

"No. I get it. You would rather have a guy that doesn't give two shits about you, and would treat you like garbage. You're right, that isn't me," Victor said, raising his eyebrows in astonishment.

"Okay. So, we're agreed, then? No reason to continue with this awkward dance."

"What awkward dance?" Victor asked.

"The one where I tell you I'm not interested, and you still continue to pursue me. I have no problems being your friend, Victor. Some things we talk about are interesting. But this…" Morgan said, motioning back and forth between them. "This will go nowhere. I will never be interested in you in that way. Capiche?"

"I read you loud and clear," Victor said, before turning and walking towards the fire escape, where he pushed the exit doors open, disappearing into the stairwell.

"Fuck!" Morgan called out in exasperation. "Can't I just hook up with someone without all the bullshit?"

At that moment, Morgan turned, and there in the elevator stood none other than Jamison Masters, leaning against the side wall. "And the hits just keep on coming." She grimaced.

"I'd be happy to close the doors and you could catch the next one. Wouldn't bother me one damned bit," Jamison announced, leaning toward the buttons.

"I think I can handle torturing myself with your presence for a couple of minutes on the ride down."

"Don't act like you're the only one irritated by this intrusion of their space," Jamison scoffed, pressing the button to hold the door opened.

"Your space? Next thing you'll tell me, you own the damned building. Please tell me you don't own the damned building?" Morgan crossed her arms.

"No, wench. I don't own the damned building. But I have been considering getting into real estate, so maybe I should look into it?" Jamison mused.

"If you buy the damned building, I'm moving the fuck out," Morgan promised.

"Don't threaten me with a good time. It's bad enough having to see your ass every day at work. I could use the reprieve at home."

"You? You think I enjoy this? Everywhere I look, there you are. I'm half tempted to take a round of antibiotics to see if I can rid myself of you." She stepped toward the elevator.

"A course of antibiotics? You seem to be the gift that keeps on giving, and antibiotics alone wouldn't rid me of you," Jamison spat, releasing the button to close the elevator doors. "You're on your own. Catch the next one."

The elevator doors closed and Morgan cussed before she, too, headed toward the stairwell to walk the two flights down to the lobby.

[LIVE •]

Morgan arrived at Smokey Row fifteen minutes after walking out the doors of the Lofts and was greeted by Kent at the entrance.

"I was going to go in and grab us a table, but it's not very busy, so there was no need. I figured I would just wait out here for you. You look great, by the way," Kent complimented.

"Sorry, I'm running behind. I had several annoying setbacks on my way out of the building."

"Oh? I'm down for some drama. Spill it!" Kent urged.

"I'm going to do my best to explain this situation without sounding egotistical, so here goes... wait, let's head inside and place our order, and then find ourselves a table. I'll fill you in on everything while we wait."

"Sounds good. After you," Kent said, holding the door open for Morgan.

Morgan walked in ahead of him and straight for the counter to place her order.

"Hey, girl," the barista smiled at Morgan. "Haven't seen you in a while. Can I get you the usual?" she asked cheerfully.

"Hey, Madison," Morgan answered. "I have been crazy busy with work. But yes, please. Two shots of espresso, though. I need the extra pick me up today."

"Coming right up," Madison answered.

"Just a second, Mads. Ah, what would you like, Kent?" Morgan asked, touching Kent's forearm, trailing her fingertips across its surface.

"I'm a simple caveman. Coffee, black. In a larger cup and I'll doctor it myself over at the to go bar."

"As you wish." Madison winked in his direction.

"Well, now. Look at you? I bet that cleft in your chin and those bushy eyebrows make all the girls swoon?" Morgan teased as she nudged her hip against his.

"Something like that." Kent smiled as his cheeks flushed, dropping a twenty on the counter.

"Blushing? Have I stumbled across a shy guy?" Morgan flirted.

"Shy, no. But compliments make me feel awkward."

"And why is that?"

"I don't know? I figure it has something to do with the fact I never really feel like I deserve them," he said as they turned toward the seating area.

"Shy and humble? That is two marks so far in your favor."

"Only two? How many marks do I need to stack the deck?"

"That depends?" Morgan fisted her hand under her chin in the thinker pose.

"On?" Kent questioned.

"On what your intentions are?" She dropped her pose and giggled.

"Oh, my intentions are anything but savory," he admitted.

"In what way?" Morgan asked, taking a seat in the chair Kent slid out for her.

"Well, considering the fact that when I met you, you were two seconds away from fingering yourself and putting it in my mouth... I'd say that my intentions are completely about the basest of needs," he leaned in, whispering in her ear.

"Mr. Adams? I'm shocked." She mocked surprise.

Kent took a seat opposite Morgan and placed his elbows on the tabletop. "You can play coy all you want, but you're not fooling me. Seeing as you know my last name, it appears you have asked some questions about me. Well, Miss Ericksson, I too had some questions of my own I needed answered."

"And? What did you find?" Morgan leaned in as if they were sharing secrets.

"Not a whole hell of a lot. Which has me with a bunch more questions. Care to fill me in?" He tapped on the tabletop.

"What do you want to know?" Morgan asked, fluttering her eyelashes.

Kent and Morgan shared small talk; the annoyances plaguing her before she left her building that day and tidbits about their lives before arriving in Des Moines. She left out the parts about her cheating ex and the engagement that barely was, but covered all the pertinent details; work mostly.

There was no doubt Morgan was a workaholic. She was doing her best to make slight changes regarding that. But, you know, baby steps.

Morgan wanted to be known by her friends as more than just a hard worker. Hopefully, within the next year, she could add "fun to be around" and "life of the party" to her repertoire, because she hated the feeling she was rigid and stuffy.

Bit by bit, she was making changes. Bit by bit, she was working to change her quality of life. Because it's like Melissa said, "All work and no play make Morgan a dull girl." And she wanted to be anything but.

This was her chance. Des Moines, and the move, gave her the opportunity to reinvent herself, and she had no intention of letting that opportunity go to waste.

The more Kent and Morgan talked about what they liked to do for fun, the more relaxed Morgan became. She got close enough to Kent that her knees touched his legs under the table, which were spread apart.

He smirked in her direction when they made contact, and that was the invitation she was looking for.

She leaned back in her chair and extended her leg, rubbing her boot up the length of Kent's leg from his ankle to the inside of his thigh.

He reached under the table and grabbed her foot, never looking away as they made eye contact across the table. "Careful now, little lady," he said in warning.

"Or what?" Morgan challenged.

"Or I'll show you just exactly what you missed out on last Thursday night."

"Promises, promises," she taunted.

"Trust me when I say my promises are never empty." He pushed her foot down and leaned forward, nothing but intensity in his eyes.

"If you'll excuse me?" Morgan said as she stood and straightened her skirt.

Kent stood and watched as she walked away.

Morgan looked over her shoulder and smirked before explaining, "I'm going to head to the ladies. I shouldn't be long. I just need to reapply my lip-gloss." She bit her lower lip, turned, and walked back toward the restrooms.

Kent was about to sit down when he realized Morgan had forgotten her purse. He picked it up and walked down the back hallway to the ladies' room.

He knocked on the door and when Morgan opened it, he lifted her purse from behind his back and said, "It'll be hard to reapply your lip-gloss without your purse."

Morgan reached out and grabbed the purse, but Kent didn't let go. "Can I assist you with something, Mr. Adams?"

"That depends," he said, looking down the hallway and then back toward the front.

"On?" she asked.

"On how bold you're wanting to be today?" His grin widened.

"Bold is my specialty," Morgan announced as she yanked the purse, pulling Kent inside the ladies' room, before reaching and locking the door behind him.

Morgan spun Kent around and pressed him against the bathroom door, dropping her purse at their feet.

She ran her fingertips from the collar of his shirt, up the length of his neck, and across his cheek to his lips. She stared into his eyes, her lips parted as she used one prominent canine to bite down on her tongue as she pulled his lip down with her fingernail. Lifting on her tiptoes, she ran her tongue across his bottom lip, biting it before she pulled away.

"That's it?" Kent asked. "That's your definition of bold?" Kent stood before Morgan, shaking his head.

He reached behind him for the door lock when Morgan slapped his hand away. "Who said I was done with you? I didn't give you permission to leave," Morgan announced.

She lowered to her knees before him, looking up the entire time.

Morgan unbuttoned the top of Kent's jeans and was lowering his zipper when he asked, "Can I help you with something?"

"No. But I figured I could help you with something," she teased, taking his zipper in her teeth and pulling it the rest of the way down.

Morgan traced the outline of his bulge with the tip of her nose, adding pressure as she moved her lips over the fabric of his boxer briefs.

Kent's cock jumped with excitement beneath the fabric as she caressed him. He leaned back against the door, his hips pressed forward, looking down into Morgan's amber eyes.

"I'll only do what you'll let me," she announced.

"You can do whatever you want to me, as long as you don't stop what you're doing with your mouth," Kent explained, banging his head back on the door when she breathed hot air over him. "Fuck!"

Morgan giggled and then released Kent's cock from where it was trapped behind his briefs. Still looking up at him, she gripped underneath his balls with one hand and grabbed his shaft with the other.

The firmness of her grip took him by surprise, and his breath caught in his throat before he released it in a hiss. "God damn, Morgan. Talk about a commanding presence. You have my full and undivided attention."

"Speaking of full," Morgan teased, rubbing the head of Kent's dick against her lips before placing it in her mouth. She drew him into the back of her throat, sweeping her tongue back and forth across the underside of his soft flesh as his hips hitched forward.

"Go slow," Kent grimaced. "That mouth is much more than I bargained for," he said.

Grasping a handful of her hair at the base of her neck, he slid himself slowly forward, as far as he could go into her mouth, tilting his hips at an angle as he did. "That's it," he coached. "I'm so fucking close. Yeah. Don't stop," he guided her. "Oh, fuck!" Kent wrapped both of his hands in Morgan's hair, forcing himself into her mouth as he came, exhaling as whimpers escaped his lips.

He was embarrassed, but didn't allow the emotion to show on his face. He'd never come that fast from head, *but this girl is God damned skilled*, he thought.

Morgan continued to suck on his cock, coaxing the rest of his satisfaction from him, not wasting a single drop.

The sensation was overwhelming, and Kent withdrew. "Morgan. Morgan, stop," he pleaded. "Oh, he is sensitive. But very appreciative," he said, looking down at Morgan, who wiped the collection of saliva that had pooled at the corner of her mouth, licking her fingers clean.

"I'm glad to be of service." Morgan smirked as she rose from her knees, straightening her skirt.

She picked up her purse from where it lay on the floor at his feet and rummaged around until she found her mouthwash and lip gloss.

Walking over to the sink, she swished the mouthwash, spitting it out before applying her gloss in the mirror.

Kent walked up behind her and rubbed his fingertips up the length of her arm as she bent forward toward the mirror.

"What now, Mr. Adams?"

"Oh, we're not done. I intend to worship you just as you have me," he grinned, meeting her eyes in the mirror.

"Is that so?" she asked, turning to face him, her ass pressed against the edge of the sink.

"It is," Kent informed her, lifting her ass onto the sink before lowering in front of her.

He ran his hands up Morgan's thighs toward her center, drawing squiggly patterns with his fingernails across her panties as he waited for her response. "Last chance before I bury my face between those beautiful stems of yours?"

"By all means, Mr. Adams. I would hate to interrupt you when you seem all too keen on being a good boy," Morgan said, looking down at him.

Praise kink? Didn't see that coming, he thought.

"I'll show you a good boy," Kent challenged before spreading Morgan's legs further apart. Kent ran his tongue from her knee cap up the length of her thighs until he reached her moist center. He took a deep breath in, appreciating the scent of her arousal. "You smell so fucking good. Now, let's see how you taste."

With one hand, Kent pulled Morgan's panties to the side and used the thumb of his other to trace circles around her opening. He pressed his thumb down on her clit and then slid it through her folds, collecting the moistness of her as he did.

As he pressed the tip of his thumb into her, Morgan gasped, tightening in response. She pulsed around his thumb, caressing it as he pressed the digit further into her. She sighed, her head falling back and banging against the mirror as her legs fell further apart, exposing her completely.

Kent withdrew his thumb and rose, standing before her. She looked up at him through lowered lashes, a pant escaping as she watched him wipe her sweetness across his lips with his thumb.

That's fucking hot, Morgan thought.

He reached out, placing his thumb on her bottom lip and said, "Taste how sweet you are."

She drew his thumb into her mouth and suckled it, circling her tongue around its length.

"I want more," he said, dropping once again to his knees, and this time pressing his entire face between her thighs. He traced his tongue along the seam of her panties as her anticipation built.

Morgan sighed, digging her fingernails into the palms of her hands where they were fisted at her side as she sat on the edge of the sink.

Kent grabbed the waistband of her underwear and drug them down over her ass, gathering them at the crook of her knees. He placed the backs of her thighs over his shoulders, his head between her legs, and moved his face to hover over her lips.

He blew gently, the sensation causing goosebumps to form across the surface of her abdomen, and traced her folds with his tongue as he grabbed her ass, pulling her against his face.

"Oh, fuck!" Morgan moaned, her head falling backward as she

sat sprawled open for him to feast upon. "That feels so fucking good."

Kent held Morgan there on the sink, her juices dripping down his chin. Her legs began to coil and constrict around him, trapping his face in place.

He eventually removed her panties, tossing them to the floor as he continued to manipulate her clit with his tongue, lapping up every drop that burst forth as she climaxed, moaning when she crested.

"Yes. Yes," she breathed heavily, biting down on her arm to muffle her cries.

Morgan ground into Kent's face, riding the waves of her satisfaction as they ebbed and flowed, giggling right after she reached climax again. When she released Kent from where she had trapped him between her thighs, he shook his head to relieve the pressure that built in his ears from the suction created by her thighs.

"Sorry." She giggled.

"Don't be sorry. I'm not," he smiled up at her, lapping up the moisture from her center one last time. "Mmmm. Oh, yeah!" He chuckled.

"Stop! No. Not Mr. Kool-Aid. Never do that again. It was cringy," she whined.

"Cringy? I thought it was hilarious," Kent said, rising before her. He lifted her ass off the sink and wrapped her legs around his waist.

"You do realize I'm soaking your shirt?" Morgan pointed out.

"It'll wash," he said. "Besides, now I can smell you all day."

The widest grin formed on her lips as she thought about him walking around with a hard on all day from smelling her pussy on him.

"Okay, then. Well, do you mind?" She pointed to where her panties lay on the floor.

Kent set her back down, releasing her legs so he could bend over to retrieve her undergarments. He handed them to her before he picked up her purse. "Do you need help putting them back on?" He lifted his brows, their bushiness reminding her so much of Groucho Marx.

"I have no intention of putting them back on," she admitted.

"Really?" he exaggerated the word. He smiled wickedly.

"Really, really."

"Okay. But, if I get distracted while we finish our coffee, you know why." He winked.

"Duly noted," she said, tucking her panties in the front pocket of her purse.

Kent and Morgan walked back into the seating area and again took their seats at the table they had left empty. Sitting on top was a fresh drink for both of them.

Morgan looked over to the barista station, where Madison blew her a kiss, giggling to herself as she wiped down the espresso machine. They finished their drinks, talked for a little while longer, and then ended their afternoon with the promise to do it again sometime—the coffee, and perhaps the sex.

Only time would tell, but thus far, Kent had distinguished himself enough for another go of it. Perhaps next time she'd upgrade him to a dinner date. Hell, maybe even an overnight. But until then, she'd keep the taste of him in the forefront of her mind, and reminisce on all the things he did with that skilled tongue of his.

CHAPTER 6

IT'S JUST LUNCH

Morgan woke early the next day and, as she was getting ready, a rather long message popped up on her phone. She thought for sure it was from Kent, but it wasn't. She didn't know the number it came from, and as she was reading through it, a look of confusion crossed her features.

Whoever the message was from was relaying moments from her night out last week and talking to her as if they were old friends. She didn't want to be rude, or admit she had no clue who it was that was messaging, so she just replied as basically as she could.

> That's just so crazy. I was just telling Nora she shouldn't be so possessive of me when we go out, and now here you are, reaching out.

I mean... I wouldn't have even had the opportunity if that bartender hadn't tried to snatch your number from your friend when he was closing out your tab. Good thing I was standing there to remind him I was going to cover it.

What a happy coincidence, indeed.

Absolutely. So, as I was saying, how would you like to join me for lunch?

I could eat. 🥺 I'm off for the weekend. As it turns out, Nora has a girls' trip planned for Olivia and I. But I can definitely meet you for lunch before I pack.

Excellent. Do you like Poké?

I love it!

Good. Do you know the place on MLK and SW 3rd?

Yeah.

I can pick you up or you can meet me there?

I'll just meet you there. It'd be easier.

And that way, if he's horrid, I have my own mode of transportation to escape; she thought.

How's 1:30 sound?

LIVE

Morgan arrived at the front steps of the restaurant and looked around. The message had said he would meet her, but there was no one about.

She pulled out her phone, and was about to message back the number for the man who contacted her that morning, when a motorcycle pulled up behind her.

Morgan turned, and as she did, a tall, slender man removed his helmet to reveal blonde hair, pierced ears, shining blue eyes, and the most handsome face she had ever seen, sitting atop a dark green, Ducati 998S. The *Matrix* version, which she only knew because it was Eric's favorite fucking movie. They'd watched it nearly one hundred times, so she'd know that bike anywhere.

"Morgan," the man said, his voice silky and smooth as he almost purred her name. He sat straddling his bike as he ran his hands through his hair, not breaking eye contact even once.

"Sir?" Morgan cooed as she raised her eyebrows at him.

"Lucas will work. Mr. Kentworth, if you're feeling formal. But for now, anyway, let's save the Sir for later, shall we?"

"As you wish." Morgan smiled.

She appraised him as his eyes made their way up and down her form. *Look at him,* she thought. *Sitting there all hot and shit with just as much bravado as Evel Knievel. Probably just as reckless, too.*

"A Ducati?" She raised a brow, stepping toward the bike. She traced the smooth fiberglass along the rear fairing. "But not just any Ducati." Morgan beamed, her fingers walking back toward the tail lights.

"Oh!" Lucas called out, reaching for her hand, but it was too late.

Morgan had absentmindedly tapped the exhaust on her way around the bike, and it was hot, which she forgot. Embarrassed, she raised her singed finger to her mouth as Lucas watched her intently. She stepped back. "This is like 'the' Ducati."

"Do you know a lot about motorcycles?" He flashed a toothy grin.

"No. But I know a lot about expensive vehicles. Call it an after-effect of being around way too much wealth and privilege." She sneered.

"Ouch! Strikes against me already, and we've just met. Well, if it helps, my other bike is a KTM 450."

"I'll give you the benefit of the doubt," she said. "At least for now. But yeah, no clue what the other bike is." She shrugged her shoulders.

"It's for Motocross. Let's call it a hobby." He placed his helmet under his arm and dismounted his bike.

"Expensive hobby."

"That it is." He motioned toward the front door of the restaurant.

Lucas Abdul Kentworth was majoring in finance at Drake University. His mother, Farah Munira Kentworth, a widow from Dubai, moved her and Lucas to the United States six years ago, when Lucas decided he wanted to race motocross professionally.

He was born in the U.S. and moved around a lot during his youth, but chose Des Moines to attend university. It was Midwestern, and close enough to the company out of Wisconsin sponsoring him, but also because he had a long-time friend attending there as well.

Farah wasn't a huge fan of the idea—the motocross or the move to the Midwest. She was used to a certain lifestyle, had specific tastes, and ambitions that living in Des Moines would hinder. Between her late husband's money and her own, she had no intentions of working anytime soon. At least not hard, anyway. So Lucas lived there while she lived in New York.

She was hoping Lucas would have the same work ethic, or lack thereof, but he was always such a busybody. He enjoyed the finer things in life, as she did, and occasionally, he too liked to have fun and flash their money around, but not in the same manner she did.

That's not to say she wasn't business minded. She wanted to run a business. Well, actually, she wanted a business named after her—Farah Beauty, a cosmetics company she selected the products for and determined how they would be marketed, but was run and managed by someone else who took care of all the daily tasks associated with running it.

She was happy to just point and nod while sipping expensive champagne. The company would be hers in name, and when the business saw profit, but otherwise, the responsibility could fall elsewhere. She had people for those kinds of things.

Lucas and Morgan entered the restaurant, and the hostess sat them near the window overlooking downtown.

"It is such a beautiful day," Lucas said. "I couldn't help but get a ride in. Do you ride?"

"Motorcycles? No," Morgan answered as she played with her straw, twirling it with her tongue. It was better than biting her nails, which is what she normally did when she was nervous.

"If not motorcycles, then what?"

Morgan choked on her water as it went down the wrong pipe. "I'm sorry?" she questioned, after she stopped choking.

"You specified no to the motorcycle question. So, what do you ride?"

Wouldn't you like to know? she thought.

Morgan laughed aloud as Lucas looked on in confusion. "I'm sorry," Morgan apologized. "I was being a smartass. I didn't intend for you to ask a follow-on question."

"And here I was asking a follow-on question, because I thought you were being cheeky. My mistake." He smiled.

"No mistake. You picked up on what I was alluding to, rather nicely. Well played."

"I'm not the one with the play on words. That was all you, gorgeous." Lucas winked.

Morgan winced. "Ugh. Please, pick a different pet name, if I must have one."

"Don't enjoy being called gorgeous?" He tilted his head with curiosity.

"Don't like the memories associated with being called gorgeous," she explained.

"I'll refrain if it makes you uncomfortable." His features turned serious.

She rolled her eyes. "It doesn't make me uncomfortable, per se. But the person who said it left a rather unpleasant taste in my mouth," Morgan said as she nervously took another drink of water.

"I promise I will never leave a foul taste in your mouth." Lucas smirked as he ran his fingertip around the rim of his glass.

Morgan again choked on her water. "You sure are full of innuendo," she said when she caught her breath.

"I can think of a few things I would like to fill."

"Stop! Okay, I get it. You're a horn ball. No need to put it on so thick," Morgan stated as she raised her eyebrows and looked away.

"I'm sorry. It appears I've gotten the wrong impression of you. And now... I've made an ass of myself."

"What impression is that, exactly?" She crossed her arms, pushing her breasts together and above the neckline of her top.

Lucas' eyes dropped to her cleavage, but quickly rose to where they were met with a glaring Morgan.

"When we met at the bar, you were all too ready to have my hands all over you, and you didn't even know my name. My apologies, but I just figured that you were eager and willing." He leaned back in his chair nonchalantly.

Morgan leaned forward, her arms braced on the tabletop as she interlaced her fingers very businesslike, and Lucas picked up on the change in her posture. "Let me get this straight: a drunk girl at the bar gets a little handsy, and in your mind, that means you can do or say whatever you want?"

"It seems we have gotten off on the wrong foot, or at least I have." He reached for her hand and she swatted him away. "Any chance you'd be willing to let me start over? I'd like the opportunity to pull my foot out of my mouth." He looked at her pleadingly. "What do you say? Give an idiot a second chance?"

Morgan pulled her arms back avoidantly, sitting with them crossed once again, but nodded her head in agreement.

With the mood shifted back to one of a casual nature, she asked, "Is it just me, or do I detect a bit of an accent?"

"I'm a U.S. citizen, but you're right. I spent a lot of time in Dubai, the UK, all over Europe and Asia, really. Try as I might, there are some remnants of one."

"Is that where you got the Ducati?"

"During my travels? Yes. From England. Sheffield, to be precise. Have you ever been?"

"Can't say I've had the pleasure. My life has been rather land locked. No stamps in my passport." She took another sip of her water as she waited for him to continue.

"Maybe we can remedy that. What do you say?"

"To travel? Count me in." She offered him a genuine smile, despite thinking his offer was bullshit.

The conversation continued, but this time Lucas and Morgan actually talked. They put the innuendo aside and discussed Morgan's plans for the weekend and her girls' trip with Nora and Olivia.

Just as they were finishing lunch, Morgan received a text message telling her that Olivia and Nora had gotten called into work, so they would have to reschedule their weekend away.

"Shit!" Morgan huffed.

"What's the matter?" Lucas asked, a genuine look of concern dressing his features.

"The girls got called in to cover for some of the catering staff who called in sick. So much for a weekend away." She moped, slouching down in her chair.

"So, your weekend is wide open?"

"It appears so."

"Care to join me, then?"

"Join you?" She raised a brow.

"I'm heading out of town after this. I have a ride in Lincoln this weekend. Motocross. I would love some company if you're up for it? I can call and get another room booked. What do you say?"

This guy is too good to be true, Morgan thought, but agreed to accompany him.

She explained she needed to go back to her apartment to grab a bag and a change of clothes, so they paid the check and left the restaurant.

Lucas followed Morgan back to the lofts, she parked her car, and as she was getting ready to go inside, Lucas mentioned his friend lived in her building.

Morgan smiled at him, but didn't ask who his friend was before she headed upstairs to pack and grab her bag. When she came back downstairs, exiting the elevator and stepping into the entryway, she saw Lucas talking to none other than Jamison Masters.

Lucas sat atop his motorcycle, leaning back as they chatted, and as Morgan exited, Jamison looked over in her direction, fake smiled, and then walked away.

Morgan walked over to Lucas, who handed her his helmet, and scooted forward so she could hop on behind him.

"Was that your friend, the one who lives in the building?" she asked as she was prepping the helmet.

"Who, Jamison? Yeah. He's my buddy. We spend little time together anymore, but we have some of the same classes together. And apparently... he does not like you."

"No," she said. "No, he does not."

Morgan positioned herself behind Lucas, wrapping her arms around his waist as they rode the several miles to his shop.

When they arrived, his team had already loaded his other bike into the back of the truck. It was black and covered in red sponsorship stickers for a company with a logo resembling a dart flight, with the company's letters emblazoned next to it. There were protective gear and storage boxes, all bearing the same logo, strapped along the walls.

Lucas rode the bike, with him and Morgan on the back, up the ramp and into the back of the truck. Once they dismounted, two men walked up the ramps and assisted Lucas in strapping his bike down.

"Geesh. With all that name branding, you'd think you had a sponsorship." She chuckled.

"I do, actually."

"Oh, my bad. I was just joking. I had no idea." Her cheeks flushed in embarrassment.

"I have a lot of money, but my mom would never be okay with me spending it on all this stuff. So, I figured sponsorship was the best route." He pulled the canvas strap taught.

"I just assumed you bought it all yourself. You must be pretty good if you have a sponsorship," Morgan said as she ran her fingers along the top of a box along the back wall. She pulled her hand back, her finger still tender from burning it earlier.

"I do alright." He smiled up at her from where he was tightening the straps fastening the front wheel of his Ducati. "My mom is..." he trailed off. "My mom is different when it comes to spending. If it's for having fun and looking good, then I can spend it all day long and she doesn't bat a single perfectly attached synthetic eyelash. But, if I even think about investing or doing something she would consider being 'work', she complains because she doesn't see the value in it. It makes little sense, and it's bass akward if you ask me."

"Bass akward?" Morgan laughed. "I thought only my mom said that."

"Well, then consider yourself in good company. Because I, too, use antiquated commentary." Finished securing his bike, Lucas stood and wiped his hands off on his pants.

She was in good company. Morgan was warming up to him, and despite where the day had begun, she was looking forward to where it seemed to be going now. And to the possibilities of what this weekend had in store for her.

Morgan had been wanting to scratch that itch, that thirst self gratification alone couldn't quench, and now, it seemed, the odds were ever in her favor.

As the men finished the preparations for their departure,

Lucas announced he and Morgan would ride in back with the bikes. It would be roomier that way; not cramming themselves into the tiny backseat of the truck for the almost three-hour drive to Lincoln.

Lucas' guys shrugged their shoulders and closed up the back before getting into the cab.

Lucas and Morgan stretched out on the benches lining the walls of the back of the truck. As she stared up at the ceiling, thinking about the plans that had gotten cancelled that day, she let out a loud sigh. "Ugh!"

He sat up and looked over to where Morgan lay on the bench, her legs bent, with her hands resting on her stomach.

"What's the matter?"

"Just frustrated. This was supposed to be a much-needed weekend away to relax and recharge, and get out of my head a little."

"So, what's stopping you? There are no definitive plans, other than the event. Everything else is at our leisure. What's it gonna take for you to let off some steam?" He stood and walked over, taking a seat on the bench beside her.

She sat up and faced him. "For starters, we were going to get spa treatments; a little pampering and a much-needed massage."

Lucas placed his hand on her knee. "We can still add that to the agenda. Tell me what you need and I can have it booked in a matter of minutes."

"I couldn't ask you to do that." Morgan looked away.

He placed his hand under her chin, turning her face toward him. "You're not asking, I'm offering," he said as he stared at her intently. He took out his phone and had his browser open as he waited. "What's it gonna be, madame?"

"Seriously?"

"I'm waiting. What am I booking?"

"Okay," she agreed, nodding her head. She ticked off on her fingers. "I need a deep tissue or hot stone massage, a facial, manicure and pedicure, and maybe a body wrap?" Holding up five fingers, she wiggled them.

"I know a place. It's phenomenal. Literally," he said, typing frantically on his phone. "Hell, I might even join you, if that's okay?"

"Sure thing." She grinned, craning her head to look at him as he looked down at his phone.

Morgan stretched her arms overhead, arching her back as she attempted to loosen it up. "Is it safe to walk around?" she asked, causing Lucas to look up from his screen.

"You should be fine. Just make sure you have hold of something as you shift your position." He locked his phone and placed it on the bench beside him.

Morgan walked over to Lucas' Ducati and ran her fingertips along the seat. "This is a thing of beauty. May I?" she asked, motioning toward his bike.

"Be my guest." He leaned back, watching her.

She moved, ensuring not to disturb the bike where it was strapped down. Straddling the seat, she asked him, "How do I look?"

"So sexy. How often is it you've had that much power between your legs?"

"Besides my toys?" Her eyes twinkled, the mischief of her reply shining brightly in their amber depths.

Lucas appraised Morgan as she gripped his seat between her thighs. She had on black leggings, a matching crop tank top, with ankle-length slide on moto boots, and a black cropped denim jacket.

"You know..." he said, rising and walking toward her. "I could do my best to help you relax now. How's a little teaser before the real spa treatment later?" He placed his hands on the seat behind her.

Lucas climbed on the back of his bike and slid Morgan towards him. He rubbed her shoulders through her jacket and she groaned as his skilled hands made short work of the tension in her neck.

"That feels amazing," she cooed.

He slowly slid her jacket off, dropping it to the floor, before running his hands over the fabric of her top. The backs of his knuckles rubbed across her nipples, and they hardened in response, her breasts forming tight peaks.

Morgan shifted her weight, lifting off the seat and spinning around to face him, draping her legs over his and sliding up into his lap.

Lucas adjusted her position, gripping underneath her thighs, and pulled her down onto his hardening length.

She sat in his lap, searching his eyes as she ran her nails up the back of his neck. In his eyes, she saw need; she saw a fire burning. And between their bodies, she felt a scorching heat. She had stoked the flames, and now she wanted to release the inferno and see just how tolerant of this burning sensation she could be.

Morgan welcomed that burn. She opened herself and laid her desire in that same lap where she now ground her pelvis against him as he hardened with each rotation of her hips.

Lucas placed his hands, one on each side of Morgan's chin, pulling her face down to his before releasing and placing his hands back on the top of her thighs. He sucked her lip into his mouth, biting down as his hands continued to wander their way back and forth across the length of her thighs, massaging the fabric of her leggings before cupping her ass in his hands.

She moaned into his mouth, causing his cock to pulse at the smooth sound of her whimpers.

He released his teeth's hold on her and took a deep breath in before he said, "I want you." His gaze was intense and his body's reaction insistent. His hands gripped and grasped her ass, rubbing her across his bulge, and her pussy clenched in response.

"I need it," Morgan announced. "I want you to fuck me."

"I will happily fuck you," Lucas answered, shifting his weight and pushing her off of him, back onto the seat.

"No." She pouted, sliding back up into his lap.

"No?"

Morgan positioned her lips at the opening of Lucas' ear. "Fuck me on the Ducati," she breathed.

"On the Ducati?" He ran his hand between them, rubbing the back of his hand over his growing erection before he cupped her heat.

"It's as you said. How often is it I have this much power between my legs?" She sighed as she ground against his hand.

Morgan lifted slightly, and Lucas' hand followed, his thumb tracing circles across the seam of her pants. His attentions sent her core to weeping, and her heat beckoned him to her.

He growled. "Oh, I will gladly fuck you on this bike."

With Morgan's legs still draped across the top of his own, Lucas reached his other hand under her, and grabbed the waistband of her leggings at the small of her back with both hands, pulling them down. Her ass was exposed, but it took one more tug forward before he could access that beautiful pink center.

Morgan sat there wide eyed, her core tensing from the anticipation of what he would do next.

Lucas fought to unfasten his jeans and release his cock from where it remained trapped. It wanted to feel her. It wanted to fill her. It wanted to be drenched and sticky, coated in her juices as he dug his nails into her cheeks.

With his cock free of the constraints of his pants, Lucas pulled

Morgan's bare ass back up into his lap. Her legs, still trapped in her leggings, he lifted, bending her in half as he rested both of them on one of his shoulders.

The head of his cock brushed against her opening, and although he was unsure what she wanted was even possible, he pulsed with excitement. Finally, driving forward, he slid through her sweetness, his head bottoming out once he was fully seated inside her.

"Fuck!" Lucas called out as he dragged Morgan back and forth along his shaft. "You are so fucking wet. And those sloppy sounds... ugh," he grimaced. "Your pussy is so God damned tight."

"You feel so fucking good," she said, gripping her nails into the backs of his biceps.

"Thank God you're flexible." He chuckled. "Otherwise, this might be difficult to accomplish."

"Wait," she said, sliding back slightly.

Lucas stopped when his tip popped out, and Morgan reached above his shoulder, sliding off her boot. She then grabbed the ankle of one legging and pulled it off, freeing her leg.

"That's better." She smiled, moving herself back into position for him to enter her again. She wrapped her free leg around his back, propped against his hip, as the other leg remained on his shoulder. "Now, go."

"Yes, ma'am," he announced. *She doesn't have to tell me twice,* he thought.

Lucas splayed her lips open with two fingers as he slipped his cock through her slick. With her legs free, now she could rock forward onto him, meeting each of his thrusts with movements of her own.

Morgan allowed her head to fall back as Lucas pulled her back and forth, the friction against her clit causing it to swell.

His breathing and the sloshing of her wetness were the only

sounds she could hear over the melodic drumming her blood pumping made in her ears. It was so loud.

With each thrust, her heart thumped louder. With each drive forward, it pounded as it thud, thud, thudded; shallow breaths escaping as her eyes screwed shut.

She was close, on the edge. He had her teetering as he built and swelled inside her.

He was ready to explode. He was ready to fill every inch and coat her walls. To splash them with his satisfaction, claiming this climax in both their names. "Morgan!" he yelled aloud. "Fuck, yes. Right there," he groaned.

Morgan cried out as her walls tightened around him. She sucked him in further with each pulse, pulled him deeper into her, where he succumbed to her charms. Into her where he could release all that innuendo and longing that had built earlier that day during lunch. And as she climaxed, she let out a short giggle.

As Lucas released one last breath into the crease of Morgan's neck, her peaked breasts pressing against him through her shirt, he stilled. They both breathed out, both continued to constrict; her around him and him inside her.

"That was…" he trailed off, barely able to get out the words.

"That was," she answered seductively. "Yes, Sir. It was." She giggled. "Ooh! Ow, my legs! Help. Help. Slowly, lower that leg, please."

Lucas assisted Morgan in lowering her leg from where she had placed it on his shoulder, and her hip popped as she did.

"Ow." He shuddered. "You okay?"

She slid off the seat and winced, rotating her hips in a circular motion before arching her back.

As Morgan dressed, she said, "More than okay. Just a little sore. Nothing a little stretching won't ease."

"Well…" Lucas said as he put himself back inside his briefs.

"Once we get to Lincoln, I'll make sure you get taken care of." He zipped his jeans and fastened the button.

"I thought you already did that?" She smirked, bending over as she continued to dress.

"Yes, well. Let me rephrase that. When we get to Lincoln, I'll make sure you get all the services you requested."

Lucas sat on the back of his bike, a look of pure satisfaction on his face. "And if I need more of YOUR services?" Morgan exaggerated, stepping up to the bike.

"I'm sure I can arrange that, as well," he said as he reached over and ran his thumb across her full bottom lip. "I can't stop after only one taste. You are just way too fucking sweet to not devour at least one more time."

"Only one more time?" She winked.

"Look, Miss Ericksson. I get it. You're a horn ball. No need to put it on so thick," he teased.

"Touché, Sir. Touché."

CHAPTER 7
IT'S JUST DRINKS

A week after her return from the amazing weekend in Lincoln with Lucas, Morgan was upstairs at the hotel, turning down the rooms for the minor league baseball team that was in house. She was setting all the informational packets on the nightstands, and the welcome gifts on the beds, when Jamison walked into the room she was prepping.

"Oh. It's you," he announced with disdain, pushing the bell cart into the room.

"Who else would it be?" she asked as he walked toward her.

"I don't know? I thought maybe one of the minor league douche bags had sent one of his groupies ahead. I guess you're kind of the same thing," he said, raising his eyebrows.

"What the fuck is that supposed to mean?" She scoffed.

"I'm just saying." He shrugged his shoulders, glancing down to her wrist where a small treble clef tattoo taunted him.

"Care to elaborate?" she asked, crossing her arms in agitation.

Jamison sat the last bag on the floor before pushing the cart toward the door.

"Nah. I'm good." He reached for the door to leave, but before he did, he stopped and said, "You can finish this up, I'm assuming?" He pushed the bell cart through the door, closing it behind him.

"Hold on just a fucking minute!" she yelled after him.

Morgan stomped across the room, throwing opened the door and entering the hallway as Jamison stepped into the elevator.

"Asshole," she muttered under her breath.

Morgan knew what happened. She was certain of it. Either Lucas filled him in on their exploits on the way to and while in Lincoln, or Kent was also one of his buddies and let their post-coffee rendezvous in the bathroom slip. Either way, she didn't give a shit about Jamison's opinion of her, or her off-the-clock activities. Her time was her own and she would spend it, however, and with whomever she saw fit. His approval be damned.

⌜LIVE•⌟

Jamison had learned a few things about Miss Morgan Ericksson since that first time he laid eyes on her those several weeks past. It took no time at all, and most of what he learned came by happenstance. In fact, the day he saw her in person for the first time hadn't been the first time he'd seen her before. It was just the first time he had seen her clothed. Despite that fact, he knew it was her.

He knew she was the one he'd been searching for. Knew she was the one that, once again, was fucking everything in his world up. She was pure evil, and if it was the last thing he did, he would see to her destruction.

Not that Jamison was obsessed with Morgan, or anything, but

he had been asking around. He had been seeking tidbits here and there to help solve the puzzle she appeared to be a key piece of.

Jamison didn't find Morgan attractive. He thought she was average compared to the women who frequented his bed.

So, what is the fascination, and why in the hell does it have to be her, of all people? he thought.

As Jamison looked back on it now, it had been four years since the last time he'd found a woman so repulsive. It was after graduation, and well into his summer following his senior year. He and his mother, Melody, had been planning a get together at their summer house. His father was still traveling for business, but had sent his assistant, Claire, out ahead of him to help him and his mother with the final preparations for their event.

The white party at the Masters' Estate was the event of the season, always had been, and all of his father's cronies, plus his mother's socialite friends, would be there.

Jamison used to hate those parties, but as he'd gotten older, he found they offered him quite the opportunity. The champagne would flow, spirits would be high, and inhibitions would be low; which allowed him to lift more than just a couple of skirts before the sun rose the next day. That year, he'd had his eyes set on Claire.

Marshall Alexander Masters and Melody Ann, what was then Duvall, met and began their courtship during their junior year at Yale. She from a prominent family in Connecticut, and he from a well-off farming family of the Midwest.

Marshall had been mild-mannered and shy when he started his freshman year as a finance student. But by the time he and Melody met at Tang, he was working on his MBA and bled navy, gold, and crimson as a member of DKE.

Melody was pursuing a degree in English and considered herself to be quite the writer. They married after graduation and moved to Robins, Iowa, where Marshall and one of his fraternity brothers, and classmates, Phillip Sorensen, went into business on their own. With their East Coast connections through Deke, and hers through her family, they had all the investment capital they needed to make a go of it.

Marshall and Phillip founded and ran their own business management company, where they "focused on operational excellence, turnaround, and restructuring, financial advisory, as well as stakeholder management," opening a second location in Florida at the height of their success.

Phillip and Marshall made a name for themselves, working and traveling most of the year, while leaving Melody to fend for herself and keep occupied.

She threw herself into writing and published her first self-help book later that year. She became the go-to for advice in her friends' group. Between her socialite friends and the women in her Pilates class, she garnered quite the following.

His mother had become, as Jamison referred to her, the "Real Housewives whisperer," spreading her guidance about self-love and self-care to all the upper-class ladies who needed no instruction on any of those things; especially since their wealth and affluence afforded them all of it.

Several years after they married, Melody and Marshall had their first and only child, Jamison. As the only grandchild of both the Duvall's and the Masters', Jamison never went without. They provided him with every opportunity to succeed, and his future seemed bright. Until that fateful summer night when his world came crashing down and his faith in his father, and the ideals of family Marshall had instilled in him, faded away to nothing.

Melody and Jamison had gone to finalize the plans for the next evening's festivities and it was always so bustling at the vineyard at that time of year. The catering company had been out at the house all morning, setting up the tents and tables, and departed when Melody and Jamison headed into town.

They left Claire to ensure the workers were out of the house because the cleaning crew would be there in a couple of hours for one last wipe down. They would be gone for a couple of hours and had informed Claire of that before they left.

Melody and Jamison had been in the car for thirty minutes when she realized she had left her wedding rings on the bathroom counter back at the house, so she had their driver turn the car around and head back.

They pulled into the circle drive in front of the house and she sent Jamison in to retrieve them. As she waited, she noticed a scuff on her heels and went into the house to change them out.

Melody stepped into the foyer and could hear raised voices coming from upstairs.

She ascended the staircase, realizing the shouting was not just Jamison's voice but that of her husband. Their voices carried down the hall and the only words she could discern were "mom" and "bastard." She had not been aware that Marshall had arrived, as he had not notified her as much.

Melody tiptoed down the hallway toward her bedroom with her heels still in her hand. She entered the room and there stood Marshall with a towel around his waist, still dripping wet from the shower as Jamison squared off with him.

Hiding away in the room's corner closest to the bathroom door was none other than Claire, wrapped in the top sheet of their bedding as she attempted to cover up the distasteful lingerie she was wearing. If she had not gasped as she looked toward the door, Melody might not have noticed her because of the scene developing in front of her.

"Marshall? What's going on?" Melody exclaimed, dropping her heels.

"Melody? I can explain," Marshall pleaded as Jamison's mother turned and walked away. "Melody! Wait!"

Marshall rushed after Melody into the hallway, stopping as she turned to face him. "How long?" she questioned as he stood there staring down at his feet. "How long?"

"It just happened," Marshall explained.

"No, Marshall. This didn't just happen. This was planned. Done to not raise any suspicions." Jamison's mother wrung her hands as she fought to wrap her head around what was happening. "I mean, why wouldn't you send your assistant out to the vineyard to help me? You couldn't be here yourself, so of course you were just being a supportive husband by allowing me the privilege of your 'employee's' skilled services." Melody sneered. "She is quite skilled, I assume? Dressed up to play the part of your fuck doll!"

"Melody, calm down," Marshall said, raising his hands as he walked toward her. He dropped them to grab his towel as it fell.

Marshall reached out for her hand. "Don't touch me!" She slapped his hand away. "Don't you fucking touch me!"

"Mom?" Jamison asked as he walked up behind his father.

"Not now, Jamison." Melody rubbed her temples.

"Can I do anything?" Jamison pleaded.

"See that Claire has all her belongings. The car will take her to the helipad. I want her on the first flight off the island."

"Okay," Jamison replied.

"Melody, that's unnecessary," Marshall stated.

"Yes, Marshall, it is indeed necessary. And Jamison..." she called out, "see that Claire understands Mr. Masters accepts her resignation."

"Understood." Jamison grinned.

"No!" Marshall interjected.

"No?" Melody responded, scowling.

"No. I am not getting rid of my assistant. She has been too much of a valuable asset."

"Oh, I'm sure. We have all gazed upon her assets today. Very valuable, indeed."

"That's enough!" Marshall raised his voice. "I give in to your whims on a lot of things. I submit to your every demand and waste godless amounts of money on your frivolity, but what I won't do is jeopardize my business."

"Your business? And what about your family?" Melody squeaked.

"My family…" Marshall said, looking back and forth between Jamison and Melody as he pointed at them, "will endure. Always has and always will."

"But at what cost?" Jamison spat.

"At whatever cost I deem appropriate!" Marshall shouted. "We have guests arriving, staff before that. You two need to suck it up because this is happening. Regardless of if you like it."

"Mom?" Jamison scowled.

"Tell him, Melody. Tell him!" Jamison's father insisted.

"Your father's right. Get Ms. Rogers set up in the pool house because I don't want to see her until I am absolutely forced to," Melody trailed off.

"Mom, no. You don't have to do this," Jamison insisted.

"Yes, Jamison. I do. And so do you. Game faces on. This will be the performance of our lives. And after it's over, I'd like to never speak of it again. Understood?"

"Mom?" Jamison whined.

"Marshall?" Melody insisted.

"Understood," Marshall said, lowering his head.

"Good. Jamison, be a good boy and do what I ask for once," Melody declared, walking into a guest room and slamming the door behind her.

"This is bullshit!" Jamison raged. He stormed off and stomped down the front stairs, slamming the front door as he exited the main house.

The memories were so clear, etched into the forefront of his mind. That bastard had destroyed his mother, broken her trust, given in to his appetites, and now it was happening all over again. But this time he would not get away with it.

$$\lceil LIVE \bullet \rfloor$$

Jamison had been visiting home two months ago, sitting on the patio with his father, when Marshall went inside for a drink. He left his phone on the table as he walked inside, and while he was gone, a photo message came in.

Jamison tapped the screen and snapped a pic of the image as his anger bubbled to the surface. "That asshole is at it again," he muttered under his breath.

He was standing to leave when his father walked back out. "Leaving so soon?"

"I've got to head back because I'm moving out of the frat house," Jamison informed him.

"Moving out? Why would you want to move out?" Marshall asked.

"Let's just say I need more privacy than the house can offer."

"Oh. I get that." His dad chuckled as he winked in his direction. "Let me know where you decide on. I have some connections in town for some real estate if you need it."

"I think I can manage," he said smugly.

Once back at his vehicle, Jamison opened the image and studied it. He would find this girl, whoever she was. He would find this tramp his dad was now fawning over; the one who

Phillip called "Nothing But Treble" in the caption below the image.

Nothing But Treble? It's catchy, but why that moniker? He was about to do an image search when he saw it. As he zoomed in on the image, attempting to discern some of the more finite details in the background and surrounding the subject, there on the woman's wrist was a small tattoo of a treble clef. And it all made sense.

"But why would Phillip and Dad call her 'Nothing But Treble'? That seems more like a screen name than a nickname," he said aloud as he sat in his Range Rover.

Thinking it couldn't be that easy, he typed the name into his search browser and sure enough, there she was. Clock app, bird app, the gram; the gang was all there. And there she was for all to see, or her breasts were.

He could see the appeal and yet, for sale or not, it was not okay his father was a customer. Jamison knew all too well the lengths his father would go to keep his playthings.

Jamison exited the elevator on the first floor of the hotel and headed straight for the lounge making a beeline for Olivia.

"Hey there, pretty lady," he flirted. "You down for drinks after work?"

"I'd love to." Olivia beamed.

Jamison tapped on the hostess podium before smiling at Olivia and walking away. It was wrong to use her in that manner, but if he'd seen another option, he would have taken it.

Olivia was giddy and cheerful but looked at Jamison a little too wide-eyed for his liking. No, she was not his type because he liked his women submissive. He liked his women seductive, showing up with a bag full of tricks and a stamina to match his own.

He liked his women like Morgan. Well, he liked his women

like "Nothing But Treble," the persona Morgan took on for her online subscribers. But as far as Morgan was concerned, his interest in her was for one purpose—taking away his father's plaything.

The lounge manager would be his in. Olivia could provide all those tiny details that would help him end this thing between Morgan and his dad.

Jamison had subscribed to Morgan's channel and followed her as soon as he found all her social media. Hell, he had even sat in on some of her live content just to see how involved she had become with his father and why he had chosen her.

It was in that space he witnessed her working her magic. Swooning and complimenting, putting it on thick as she stroked the ego of all those paying tribute.

One such subscriber, who paid tribute without hesitation, was none other than Mr. Moneybags: Scrooge McDuck. At least that was the image the person used for their profile.

It was none other than Jamison's father. He was certain of it. It was the show his father talked about watching with his college buddies as they sat around the frat house getting high and working on statistics as the intro music for *Duck Tales* played in the background.

"I see you, Mr. Moneybags," Jamison said aloud to himself that first time he was in the live. "I see you and I've got your number. Time to take away your toy, old man."

Olivia clocked out later that evening and met Jamison at the bar. With some of their other coworkers, she tossed a few back while they chatted with Seth as he tended the bar.

A few drinks later and she was getting touchy with Jamison, running her fingertips up and down the length of his arms as she licked her lips.

He smiled back at her, gripping the underside of her thighs underneath the bar as they sat socializing.

When the night ended, and they said goodbye to their friends, Jamison walked Olivia to her car. "Are you sure you should drive?"

"Why, Mr. Masters? How kind of you to be concerned about me, but I assure you I can take care of myself."

"Oh, I don't doubt that." He smirked.

"What about you?" she mused.

"Me? I can take care of myself as well." He chuckled.

"No," Olivia said as she pressed Jamison back against her car, pinning him in place. "I'm asking if you think I can take care of you?"

"Take care of me?" He laughed. "I think you've had one too many, Olivia. Why would you want to take care of me?"

Olivia slid her hands down Jamison's chest and shoved one down his pants as the other gripped the collar of his shirt.

This had not been part of Jamison's plan but might as well kill two birds with one stone: satiate the need that too long without a rendezvous had created and ply Olivia for information on Miss "Nothing But Treble." It may have started as just drinks, but the night was looking way up.

CHAPTER 8
IT'S JUST DINNER

A text came in on Morgan's phone, and as she read what Lucas sent, she smiled.

Lucas had been a pleasant surprise. He was nothing like she expected after the shambles of a lunch date they started with.

They had finished lunch that day and then spent an action-packed weekend together. There had been delightful conversation, amazing food, and mind-blowing sex. All in all, she could say she didn't regret meeting him.

He had been messaging her since they got back from Lincoln,

which was a pleasant break from the monotony because her life had been rather devoid of excitement as of late.

Since their coffee date, Kent hadn't reached out to her. She was still waiting for the notification regarding her final photoshoot for SSC Intimates, and Mr. Moneybags hadn't been around for several days.

She did, however, have a new subscriber who'd started interacting with her. He didn't offer near the amount of tributes Mr. Moneybags did, but his messages had her intrigued.

"Well, well. 'Twisted Mister'? That is an interesting name," she flirted in the DM she sent back to the subscriber who'd sent her a generous tribute. "I know there is a story behind it?"

"Aren't I supposed to be the one asking questions?" they typed.

"I suppose. But I prefer my contact to not be one sided. You were generous with your offering, and, to be honest, you've got me a little curious."

"About?"

"You. I'm curious about what you like?"

"It's all in the name, sweet cheeks. I like things twisted. I like them bound. I like them blindfolded. I like them contorted and bent to my will," Twisted Mister replied.

"And the 'them' you are referring to? Does that indicate your sexuality is fluid?"

"Not necessarily. The 'them' I refer to are my sex partners. Women, all of them. But I'm open if the situation presents itself," they answered.

"How many play partners do you have?"

"I am in between play partners at the moment."

"Then what is this?" she asked. "Do you not play when you are here?"

"I watch while I am here. I observe, and I wait."

"Wait for what?"

"For your curiosity to build enough, I sparked your interest."

"Who said I am interested?" she teased.

"Who said you weren't?"

"Now, now, Sir. You're making assumptions."

"Am I?" they asked.

"You are, indeed."

"And what assumptions are those?"

"You are assuming I communicate with all my followers," she stated.

"I never said that."

"No. But you said you were waiting for my interest to be sparked."

"And has it been?" they asked.

"No."

"No?"

"Not one bit," she said.

"Then why are you here?" they questioned.

"Just being a good hostess."

"Is that what you're doing?"

"Exactly."

They bantered back and forth through her DMs for hours on her spicy page before they switched apps. She wasn't sure which app he perused to find her, but most of her messaging happened on the gram.

As the evening wound down and her interest in him subsided, she called it a night. She relayed how she hoped to chat with him again or see him in her lives but next time he had better share some more about what he wanted to see because knowing what he wanted was important.

Morgan strived to keep the customer satisfied because, at the very heart of it, she was in the customer service industry and she aimed to please.

⌈LIVE •⌉

The next morning as Morgan was clocking in, Jamison walked into the break room. "Haven't gotten rid of you yet, I see?" Morgan grinned.

"It's like you're not even trying," Jamison teased.

"Oh, I'm not. I do my best to forget you exist, let alone that you work here."

He stopped. "And that, in and of itself, just tells me how much I'm on your mind," he called over his shoulder before turning and stepping toward her.

"Ugh. Not a chance." She gagged, pushing him back.

Just as Morgan was getting ready to leave the break room, Allison walked in and squealed. "Eek! It's just so exciting."

"Keep it down, girl," Morgan insisted. "You did a number on my ears just then."

"I'm sorry. I just can't contain myself. Never in a million years would I have thought she would have picked you."

"Thanks for the vote of confidence." Morgan rolled her eyes.

"No. I'm sorry. That came across wrong. It's just... oh, never mind."

"What was it that someone was foolish enough to pick her for?" Jamison asked.

"Don't ask about matters above your pay grade." Morgan scowled.

"Is there some military service I'm unaware of? Pay grade, really?" Jamison left the break room as Allison and Morgan continued to chat amongst themselves.

Allison filled Morgan in on what the sets were going to look like and the overall theme her boss was going for.

When Morgan and Allison left the break room some thirty minutes later, they ran right into Jamison as he turned the corner.

"Eavesdropping, really? Don't you have somewhere to be?" Morgan questioned him.

"I was thinking the exact same thing. What is it they pay you to do, anyway?" He scowled.

"Ha, ha. I do what is required of me."

"And what might that be? As far as I can tell, you are a glorified maid who turns down the beds and puts chocolates on the pillows. Anyone can do that."

"Then, by all means, if you aren't doing anything, you can follow along and I will put you to work." Morgan motioned for him to come with her finger.

"Can't," Jamison announced. "Some of us have 'real' work to do."

"Oh, yeah? Let me know when you decide to do some," Morgan called after him as he walked away.

"So, who fucked whom and didn't call the next day?" Allison asked as she looked back and forth between Morgan and Jamison's retreating silhouette.

"I beg your fucking pardon?" Morgan asked, raising her voice.

"Not a chance in hell!" Jamison assured her, his voice echoing down the back hallway.

"You're welcome." Allison grinned as she bumped into Morgan's shoulder.

"For what?"

"Getting rid of him. It's obvious you two loathe one another. At least, I think? Unless it's all an act. Please tell me it's all an act and you actually have a torrid love affair where you tie each other up on the regular? Ooh, that would be so hot." Allison smiled gleefully, swaying side to side.

"Careful. You are walking a thin line today, Miss Sims. Why don't you find your way back up to the catering closet?" As Allison turned and walked away, Morgan called after her, "Fold some linens while you're up there!"

"Fine! You're no fun," Allison trailed off as she walked away.

"So I've heard," Morgan muttered.

Several hours later, Jamison walked into the catering closet where Allison was arranging the carts for a meeting the next day in the Truman room. "If it isn't the bellboy of the hour," Allison teased.

"Funny girl. So as I was saying, inquiring minds want to know. What was Morgan chosen for?" He placed his hand on the cart she was attempting to push past him, stopping her.

"Nope. Not gonna happen. My lips are sealed." Allison pushed harder, but the cart didn't move.

"Oh, yeah?" Jamison pulled the cart toward him.

"Yup." Allison let go of the cart, stepping back.

Jamison pulled out his phone, unlocked it, and set it down on the cart in front of Allison.

"What am I supposed to do with that?"

"Your lips can stay sealed all they want, but that smirk on your face tells me you are dying for those fingers to tell me the tale. Spill it!"

Allison reluctantly picked up Jamison's phone and typed in her number, set it down on the counter beside her, and then pushed the cart away.

"Hey!" Jamison called after her. "What gives? You just sent a message?"

As Jamison stepped out of the elevator on the first floor

several minutes later, he received a text message with a link from the number Allison put in his phone. He clicked on it and it took him to a signup page where "Last Chance" scrolled across the screen.

Jamison read over the details, shocked by his good luck, and by the interesting opportunity that presented itself. He just kept finding himself doing things that weren't in the plan, but the closer he could get to Morgan, the better. And he couldn't get much closer than that.

Later that evening, with a couple of suggestive photos and a seductive introduction video submitted, Jamison was now in the running to be the next face of SSC Intimates. All the previous male candidates hadn't hit the mark, so they opened submissions back up for a second round.

Morgan might not like him, but he would place himself into every one of her spaces until he could stop his father from spending money on her.

$$\lceil \text{LIVE} \bullet \rceil$$

Lucas arrived to pick Morgan up from her loft at seven o'clock. She invited him in to wait as she finished getting ready and he stood looking around her place as she put the finishing touches to her makeup in the bathroom.

He walked aimlessly, trying not to be too nosey, but also taking in as much as he could to see if there was anything he could use to spark a conversation later.

As he was nosing around, he noticed what looked like a backdrop of some sort tucked away in the room's corner with a ring light close to it.

"Huh?" he said to himself.

Just as the hushed words escaped his lips, Morgan walked in. "What?" she asked, stopping in her tracks.

"It's nothing. I was just looking at the ring light and thinking to myself, you don't seem like the social media type." He pointed to the corner. "Are you active?"

"Kinda," she answered uncomfortably.

"What platforms are you on?"

"I mean… I wouldn't say I'm active. But I have a couple of accounts."

"A couple?"

"Yeah. I dabble, mostly," she said as she grabbed her clutch off the side table.

"Anything cool I might enjoy?" he pried.

"Probably not," she said, avoiding making eye contact.

"I get it. It's okay. You don't need to share if it's too invasive."

"That's not it," she assured him.

"I know people use social media sometimes to put on an act, and that they are nothing like their online presence. It's cool."

Morgan just smiled and said, "Well, I am ready. Should we go?"

Lucas escorted Morgan into the hallway, where they silently waited for the elevator. Victor walked out of his apartment, stopped, and shook his head.

"What?" Morgan asked, crossing her arms.

"Nothing," Victor said, his eyes widening.

"Say it!" she demanded.

"There's nothing to say." He shrugged his shoulders dismissively.

"Your face says otherwise."

"It's just… another one?" He pointed at Lucas.

"Not that it's any of your business. Look, I don't need your approval to live my life or to hang out with whoever I see fit. So if you have thoughts or an opinion on the matter, save it."

Victor walked back into his apartment and slammed the door behind him.

Morgan and Lucas entered the elevator when the doors opened and stood quietly as the lift descended.

"Do I even want to ask what that was all about?" Lucas pressed, looking over at Morgan.

"That was the aftereffects of a mistake I made early in my residence here. One I am desperately trying to shake."

"Ah," Lucas acknowledged. "Yeah, I've had one of those before, too. Hard to shake, those are."

"Any chance we'll run into one of yours while we're out?"

"Not likely. We're safe as long as we don't take a trip to Ibiza."

Lucas and Morgan chuckled, exiting the elevator on the first floor. He then led her to his Mercedes C 63 parked out front.

"This is nice," she said.

"Thanks. It's my daily driver," he said as he opened the door for her.

"Your daily driver? How many cars do you have?" she asked as she climbed in.

He closed the door behind her and then climbed into the driver's seat and replied, "In the states?"

"No, inter-galactically. Yes, in the states?"

"Twelve, currently. But I'm in the market for an Actros 1846."

"What is an Actros?"

"Look it up," Lucas instructed.

Morgan opened the browser on her phone and began her search. A large semi-looking vehicle came up. "You want a semi?"

"Kinda. Now add Vario to the search," he prompted, pointing to her screen.

The new search criteria loaded and she gasped. "1.2 million dollars! You can't be serious?"

"Go big or go home." He laughed.

As she fastened her seat belt, she watched the video about the specs and customization options. "You can build this thing however you want!" she exclaimed.

Lucas pulled out of the parking space and navigated downtown as they continued to talk about all the things he wanted in his Mobil order. By the time they pulled up at the restaurant, Morgan had put a tally on all the up sales and add-ons, and his price tag went well beyond the original estimate they discussed.

"Okay, so 1.2 million is a lot of money. But what you are talking about is insanity... and you wouldn't even be able to bring it here."

"I know. But I like to travel to Europe so it saves me on hotels and rental cars. Plus, my mom would be all for me spending some of my money on something frivolous."

"I knew you had money, but that's stupid money." She sat wide-eyed.

"Yes, and I sometimes do stupid things with my stupid money." He tried to be cool but laughed when he saw how wide her eyes were.

[LIVE•]

They arrived at the restaurant and the maître d' sat them at a quiet table. The whole restaurant was dark stained wood, an almost mahogany color, with muted lighting that created a sophisticated ambiance.

When their waiter arrived, Morgan ordered pancetta wrapped scallops with a red pepper glaze to start, and a wedge salad, while

Lucas opted to go with the bone-in Delmonico and mushroom pan roast. He was a huge fan of cheese and boasted about how they baked the mushrooms with Boursin and parmesan.

A little taken aback by the prices, Morgan fought her frugality by opting for filet medallions with the lobster claw and veal demi-glace as her main course, leaving the wine choice to Lucas.

Once their starters were delivered, Lucas ordered a bottle of Château Lafite for them to share.

"There's that stupid money again," she smiled as she watched the waiter prepare their glasses.

Morgan took a big whiff, allowing her senses to prepare her for that first sip. "Oh, that's fucking good," she gushed. "Excuse me." She blushed. "This is excellent." She smiled genuinely up at their waiter and then over at Lucas.

"It's okay if you're not a wine person," he mused. "But I think everyone should experience a Rothschild at least once in their life."

"Yeah, well. You have champagne tastes and caviar dreams, while I'm over here rocking a box wine budget." She took another sip from her glass.

Lucas and Morgan finished their meal, and when their waiter came asking about dessert, they declined.

As Lucas waited for the check, he and Morgan kept glancing across the table at one another. She would smirk and he would raise his eyebrows and smile.

"I'm surprised you passed on dessert. You seem to like every-thing on the menu," Morgan pointed out.

"I like this place, don't get me wrong. But what I had in mind for dessert isn't on the menu."

Morgan blushed, but tried to play it off by saying, "Does wine make you flush, too?"

After leaving the restaurant, Lucas opened the door to his car and, as Morgan was getting in, he asked, "How would you like to come back to my place for a nightcap?"

"I'd like that." She smiled, and he closed the door before getting in on the driver's side.

They drove in silence while Lucas stole looks over at Morgan several times along the way.

Several minutes later, he pulled into a garage at the bottom of a large brick building that looked more like an office building than a residence. "Where are we?" she asked as she got out of the car and looked around.

"My place."

"I've driven by here before, but I did not know it was a residential space."

"It's not, exactly. I'm converting it into a showroom for my bikes, but I live on the upper level. And the best part is I have a rooftop patio with an excellent view."

Lucas gave Morgan the grand tour, highlighting all the key features: kitchen, bathroom, and, of the course, the bedroom.

They stood in his kitchen for several minutes, Morgan taking in and judging his tile selection as Lucas made them both a drink: whiskey neat.

She took a sip and then followed Lucas out to the patio. "This is nice," Morgan appraised.

"Thanks. I wanted as much open air as possible but also some privacy if I had visitors."

"Visitors?" Morgan asked. "You mean women."

"I mean visitors." Lucas winked.

"Oh, okay. Duly noted."

"It's not something that is common knowledge. And I don't

advertise as such, but I consider myself to be very equal opportunity."

"I learn something new about you every day." She smiled.

Lucas and Morgan lounged on his patio, sipping on their drinks as they enjoyed the night air.

"You don't have to sit so far away. I don't bite," Lucas joked.

Morgan got up from where she sat on the lounger and joined him on the loveseat on the other side of the fire table. "There, is that better?"

"Much," he said as he reached around her, grabbed her hip, and pulled her body against his.

She snuggled into the crook of his shoulder as they talked about their thoughts of the city and how long she thought she might stay. They chatted about literature and films and he was more well-read than she imagined, stating his favorite book was *Robinson Crusoe.*

"Why do you love that one when there are so many others to choose from?"

"What's not to love? Cannibals, captives, mutineers, and a man running away from his family's expectations to make a life for himself?"

"Yes, but his best laid plans kept ending in tragedy, one after another."

"True. But at some point, you have to fend for yourself and make the best out of whatever happens."

"Let's just agree to disagree."

"No disagreement. Just differing opinions. Neither is wrong," Lucas said.

"You know, you are not what I expected." She snuggled closer.

"Is that so?" He kissed the top of her head affectionately.

"After the lunch that almost ended abruptly..."

"Wait, what?" He leaned back, looking down at her expectantly.

"Oh, yeah. I was one lewd remark away from walking out the door."

"Seriously? Miss innuendo herself? My commentary turned you off?" he asked, offended.

"Don't get your panties in a bunch. You redeemed yourself."

"I redeemed myself? You jumped my bones in the back of a moving truck!"

"And you enjoyed every minute!" she exclaimed.

"True. But were you seriously considering leaving after some harmless innuendo and flirtation?"

"I thought about it." Morgan sipped her drink, her eyes twinkling as she flirted with him.

"It's a good thing you didn't."

"And why's that?"

"You would've missed out on the best fucking of your life." He squeezed her tighter.

"And there it went." She chuckled.

"What?" He grinned.

Morgan stood and walked over to the railing at the edge of the patio, looking down at the sidewalk below. "There it is," she pointed. "You left your dignity entering your building." She laughed heartily.

Lucas stood, staring smugly at Morgan as he walked up behind her. He smacked her hard on her ass. "You're an ass, you know that?"

"Yes, but you like my ass."

"Oh, I really do. And I like how that ass moves when you're riding my dick."

Morgan pushed back against him, sashaying her hips back and forth as her cheeks rubbed against the front of his pants. She reached behind her and grabbed his dick through his pants, looking over her shoulder at him. "Speaking of riding? How about we go inside?"

"Maybe for round two."

"Round two?"

"Round one begins now," Lucas said as he ran his hand down along her waist, cupping her in his hands when he reached her crotch.

Lucas grasped Morgan by the throat as he began scraping his teeth along the line of her neck. His hand moved backward from the warmth of her pussy, over her hip and in between them as he bunched up her skirt in his hand at her lower back, tucking it in the band of her thong.

Pressing himself against her, he panted in her ear. "Don't move. I have plans for you."

"Is that so?" she said breathlessly.

Lucas unfastened his jeans, shimmying them down to his ankles, where he stepped out of them. He strode forward, brushing his nakedness against her bare cheeks. He moved the lace thong she was wearing to the side, exposing her moist center to the cool night air.

Her skin reacted as a shiver ran down her spine, and goose-bumps formed on her thighs. He lowered himself to one knee, grabbing her ass in his hands, and spread them apart. "That's a beautiful fucking sight," he said, burying his face in her ass.

Lucas' tongue traced the line between her cheeks, circling her entrance as she moaned out. He pulsed his tongue in and out of her opening, drawing her excitement into his mouth so he could savor her succulence.

He complimented her, "Do you have any idea how fucking good you taste?"

Lucas stood and swiped his hand through her slick, collecting her sticky sweetness, and wiped it across his dick before he pressed forward into her. He pushed himself into her as far as he could go, clutching her hips as he did.

He withdrew and whispered, "Now, come taste dessert off my cock."

Morgan turned to face him, grinning before lowering to her knees. She looked up into his eyes as she trailed her tongue up his shaft, circling the tip. She allowed her hands to wander to that sweet center between her creases, where she dripped with anticipation. Her index and forefinger circled her clit as she continued to lap up her decadence off the length of him.

As Morgan drew Lucas into her mouth, he wrapped his fists in her hair at the base of her neck, pulling her forward. He managed the pace and depth to which he thrust into the warmth of her. He controlled the angle and pressure to which his cock tickled the back of her throat, and expertly manipulated himself within her warmth as she increased her suction.

They matched one another's rhythm, their movements like a dance—one that had both partners circling in unison as their bodies reacted to an unheard tune.

As he would drive forward, she would angle and open her jaw. When he would withdraw, she would zig zag her tongue along the underside of his dick. And as he grasped her head when he neared the pinnacle, she drew her cheeks inward, sucking him harder.

He wasn't ready, and would not give in just yet. He had more in store for her, and this was just supposed to be a taste.

That is what he had directed her to do—just a taste. Just a sampling of her own sweetness from him and nothing more.

Lucas withdrew and released his fists from Morgan's hair before he reached the top. Morgan looked up, stunned and obviously disappointed.

"Oh..." Lucas said, "you didn't think I was going to let you take it, did you? You can have it, just not yet. I have more in store for us before you get a taste of me."

Lucas offered Morgan a hand, clasping her wrist as she stood. He turned and led her back under the canopy, where he threw down one of the patio cushions. He directed her to lie down and positioned his face between her thighs, sliding her thong down her legs and over her beautiful feet.

"I hadn't finished dessert yet," he announced. "Apparently, I also need to redeem myself? And somehow collect my dignity?" he mused. "Let me know if I succeed, will you?" he teased as he latched onto her clit and sucked fervently.

Morgan reached orgasm more than once, giggling each time as she glazed every inch of Lucas' face from the tip of his nose down to his chin where she dripped off of him.

Once her breathing slowed, and her chest stopped rising and falling in quick spasms, she drew her knees into her. She rocked back and forth, sitting up, and stared in wonder before she crawled toward him.

Morgan squatted over Lucas, placed his cock at her opening, and gradually lowered herself until she took in his full length.

He breathed out a sigh as he bit his lower lip. "So fucking tight. God damn, girl. I can feel you envelop every inch as your lips squeeze and pull me deeper," he complimented.

Morgan rode Lucas on that patio for the better part of an hour. He came once and then recovered for the next bout.

They eventually moved inside, Lucas throwing her over his shoulder as he stomped bare assed through his apartment to the bedroom, where he tossed her onto the center of his bed.

In the bedroom, their bodies twisted and turned, contorted

and writhed as they coaxed one climax after another from each other, ending the night as a pair of sweat drenched figures laying spent in one another's arms.

"Well?" Lucas asked as he caught his breath.

"Well, what?" Morgan exhaled.

"Did I succeed?"

"In?" she asked.

"In collecting my dignity?" he teased as he bit down on Morgan's shoulder before smacking her ass.

"What was that for?" she pouted, rubbing her blistered cheek.

"That was for doubting me in the first place."

"Well, I guess you showed me," she quipped.

"No. Not yet. But I have all night to do just that."

CHAPTER 9

IT'S JUST SEX

Olivia raised her voice as her frustration peaked, "I feel like you've just been wasting my fucking time!" She continued to dress, yanking her t-shirt over her head as she huffed.

"How do you figure?" Jamison stated calmly from where he sat naked in his bed. "I've never led you to believe this was anything more than just a casual thing. How am I somehow responsible for you misunderstanding this dynamic and developing stronger feelings?"

"Really? You're just going to claim ignorance to my feelings? I'm not affectionate with people and you allowed me to be with you. You accepted my advances and encouraged them, making me think this was going somewhere."

"It is going somewhere, or at least you are. Home. You are going home. Look, I never intended to be misleading, but this miscommunication is under no circumstances my fault," Jamison stated coldly.

"Are you kidding me? You're acting like I'm this naïve little girl who didn't understand your intentions. Apparently, it was all just a game to you!"

"You're being childish, Olivia. I never treated this like a game. We enjoyed each other but I can't change what is. I'm sorry if that doesn't fit the narrative you've created in your head, but I can't be responsible for your over inflated sense of reality."

"You're unbelievable! You took advantage of this situation and me. You could tell I wanted something more. I know you did. But despite that, you capitalized on my vulnerability. I deserve better than someone who does that."

"Then, by all means, go find them. I didn't use you. We both consented to what we were doing. I can't be responsible for the way you feel now because I never promised you anything. Hell, I didn't even allude to there being anything more. I send your ass home every time."

"No. No, you're right. You promised nothing. But your actions led me to believe there was potential for more!"

"How do you figure? I never led you to believe I wanted a serious commitment. We had fun together, and that's what I thought we both wanted," Jamison asserted.

"Fun? Is that all it was?" Olivia's voice quivered.

"It was fun. Until now, that is. You're twisting things to make me the bad guy. We are both adults; I am responsible for my feelings and you for yours."

"You're not even going to take any responsibility for the pain you've caused me? Morgan was right. You are an asshole. I hope you enjoy your shallow, casual relationships because that's all you'll ever have!"

"Spare me the lecture about how you don't agree with how I choose to live MY life," Jamison inflected. "I am fine, being friends. I am fine with having benefits in this relationship. But that's all I want. I'm sorry you misunderstood that."

"The only thing I misunderstood was how self-centered you truly are!" She stomped off, slamming the door behind her.

"Olivia! Comeback! I said I was sorry!" Jamison shouted as he stood in his doorway with a towel around his waist as Olivia fled down the stairwell. "Fuck!"

[LIVE•]

Olivia and Jamison had been hooking up for weeks. They had established a pattern of sorts: either he or she would get done with work and clock out, waiting in the lounge for the other to finish their shift. Then they would visit with Seth over several rounds before driving or Ubering back to the lofts. Once there, Jamison would undress Olivia and man handle her a bit before fucking her until she could barely breathe. The two would lie in his bed before he would call her a car and send her on her way.

Jamison was filling a void with Olivia. He wasn't being fully satisfied by their trysts, but at least he could cum and clear out some of the baby batter on his brain, getting by until the next time.

Every time Olivia would leave, Jamison would hop into Morgan's live and finish what Olivia awakened. He would watch her fondle herself, pinching her nipples as she cried out with the sheer ecstasy of the pain she would deliver, and he would imagine himself placing clamps on those perky nipples, pulling them off abruptly as she arched her back in response. And, just when he was on the verge, none other than Mr. Moneybags would pop in and start showering her with tributes, totally killing any chance he had at finishing himself off.

"He's just so fucking obvious!" Jamison would complain

through gritted teeth. "No originality, whatsoever. Same moves. Repeating the same plays over and over as he did with Claire."

Jamison lost his appetite for satisfaction after Mr. Moneybags entered the room. He couldn't focus when he knew just how much of his family's money was being spent on this woman his father had never met. Or so he hoped. He wasn't sure if they had ever met, but his plans for Miss Ericksson, and his interference with his father's affairs, depended on it.

CHAPTER 10

WASN'T SUPPOSED TO HAPPEN

"I know, Melissa," Morgan sighed. "It was a lapse in judgement. Yes, my lapses in judgement aren't normally this egregious. I am fully aware of that fact. I know. Look, this is a mistake that doesn't seem to be going away, so I might as well just grin and bear it. No, there will not be a repeat performance. Why not?" she raised her voice into her phone. "Because I am already dealing with a stage five clinger situation. I don't need to tempt the fates and send his stalker ass into full ownership mode. It's bad enough he seems to lurk around every corner when I leave my loft. I agree. If it gets too bad, I will address the issue head on. I'll just be a bitch. I can be a bitch if I have to," she argued. "Fine," she exaggerated. "I said fine! Okay. Love you, too. Yes, yes. Bitches for life. Yeah. Talk to you later. Byeee!"

Morgan thought back to the night she made the mistake that she and Melissa continue to talk about at least once a day since she'd made it.

She had just started unloading her stuff off the truck, transporting the boxes one dolly full at a time to the second floor, when another resident of her building offered to give her a hand. She wasn't one for being a damsel in distress, but she was in over her head, moving everything herself, and she knew it.

His offer of help seemed harmless, as did he. How could she have known there was something off with the man? Was she somehow expected to have a sixth sense that would alert her to his level of crazy? No. And yet, Melissa talked down to her as if she were a child who needed scolding for that misjudgment. She got it; she fucked up. And she was paying dearly for that fuck up. At least for the unforeseeable future.

The man had been exiting the elevator, on his way out of the building, as Morgan was struggling with yet another dolly full of boxes. As she opened the main glass doors, backing in as she pulled the dolly through, the wheels got caught on the door track, sending her tumbling backward.

Being the good Samaritan he was, he reached out and caught Morgan before she landed ass first on the marble floor. "Careful," he said. "That load is taller than you are. And weighs more, if I had to guess?"

"Excuse me?" Morgan said, offended, as she regained her footing.

"Oh... I. I didn't mean that negatively. I was just saying-"

"I know what you were just saying. Thank you very much," she interrupted.

"I think we've gotten off on the wrong foot. I feel terrible and I would be honored if you'd allow me to help, Mrs.?"

"It's Miss," she said dismissively as she continued to pick up her boxes that lay strewn about.

"Well, Miss. I really do just want to help," he pleaded.

"I guess there's no harm in accepting a hand from a neighbor." She smiled sheepishly.

"No harm at all." The man smiled back. "Cross my heart." He gestured.

"That's unnecessary. But... okay. Thank you...?" She left it open as a question.

"Oh! That's a question. Victor. The name's Victor Saucedo. At your service, Miss..."

"Morgan. Just Morgan is fine."

"Okay, Morgan." He smiled. "Let's get you moved in and settled, shall we?"

"Yes," she agreed warily. "Let's."

Victor assisted Morgan upstairs, helping her tote boxes from one side of her space to the other, as she began arranging furniture and attempting to figure out just how she should design the layout. She had little in the way of furnishings: a bed, several bookshelves, some small night stands, and an antique chaise lounge.

"This piece is amazing," Victor complimented as he pushed the chaise toward the center of the room.

"Thanks," Morgan accepted. "I salvaged it from the refuse."

"No way?" Victor replied in an over-the-top display of disbelief.

Morgan turned away and rolled her eyes. "Yeah," she continued, her voice echoing as she walked toward the kitchen area, and then back again. "The property I was working at did an entire remodel and changed the direction they were going with their aesthetic, so this beauty..." she plopped down on her chaise, stretching out gracefully, "became all mine."

"Well, that's awesome. You know, good things come to those who wait. That was one of my mom's favorite sayings."

"Positive affirmations aren't really my thing." She grimaced.

"No matter. I'm sure I can be positive enough for the both of us."

This dude is weird. I've known him all of twenty-five minutes and he's already talking about his mom and there being an us? Danger. Danger, Will Robinson.

Morgan's spidey senses were tingling, and she should have listened to them, but no. What did she do instead? Like a jackass, she gave him the benefit of the doubt. And that ladies and gentlemen would be the first mistake, in a series of mistakes, involving Victor Saucedo that poor Morgan would not soon forget.

Every time Morgan would pull something out of one of her knick-knack boxes, there he was reaching for the item and staring at her intently as he waited for her to direct him where to put it.

"We work well together, don't we?"

She allowed it to be a rhetorical question, not answering as she went about her business.

He walked closer to her and spoke up slightly, "I said we work well together, don't we?"

"Why are you shouting at me?" Morgan backed up, looking at him, appalled.

"Oh. I thought maybe you might be hard of hearing, so I repeated the question louder. I didn't think you'd heard me the first time."

"No, I heard you just fine. I guess I didn't understand you intended that I answer. Questions like that are normally rhetorical."

"Ha-ha. No. I rarely ask if I expect to get no answer. What would be the point of that?" He shook his head.

"What, indeed?"

That whole afternoon, every interaction was awkward, his responses and reactions seeming incredibly forced.

Who the fuck is this guy?

Morgan couldn't handle much more. She appreciated the help, but everything else she could do without entirely.

She sauntered over to her bar cart Victor had just arranged in height order and grabbed her decanter and a glass. She walked to the chaise lounge and, as she sat and poured herself a glass, Victor walked over and took it from her. "Here," he said as he pulled the decanter out of her hands. "Allow me?"

The look on her face had to have shown how taken aback she was, because Victor quickly poured her drink, set the glass on the table next to her, and walked the drink container back to the cart where he arranged it back in the order he'd had it.

He scooted it twice, the second time checking the finger spacing between that item and the next.

"Have I done something wrong?" Victor stood across the room, wringing his hands anxiously as he awaited her reply.

"No. Not at all. You know, I think I'm gonna take a little nap. All this moving has me wiped out."

"Oh, that's a good idea. You take a nap and I'll come get you in a couple of hours and we can get some dinner. What do you say?"

"We'll see." She forced a smile.

"Okay, good. I'll be back in a couple of hours."

Victor left Morgan's and as she closed the door, she mouthed to herself, "What the fuck?"

Morgan didn't know what it was about her, but she always seemed to find herself the weird ones. Drawn to her like a moth to a flame. No matter where she went, or who she met, there was always that one, usually a guy, who would make it their life's mission to follow her around like a puppy dog. And apparently, Victor was her new foster.

. . .

Several hours later, like clockwork, Victor knocked on Morgan's door. She contemplated not answering at all, and considered remaining silent, hoping he would just go away. But that guy... that guy was persistent. He wasn't the type to throw in the towel that easily.

Victor knocked three times at first, rocking back and forth on his feet as he stood with his hands in his pockets out in the hall-way. He looked around him as if he expected someone to come up behind him, focusing on the trim around her doorway as he waited.

He knocked a second time, somewhat louder this go around while Morgan peered through her spy hole, watching as she groaned on her side of the door.

She stared as he bounced up and down nervously, and then he leaned toward the door, his face becoming abnormally large in the peephole. "Morgan?" he called out, tilting his ear toward the door as he listened for any signs of movement inside. "Are you home? It's me, Victor."

Morgan huffed, put on her best customer service face, and opened her door. "Victor," she feigned excitement. "It's you."

"It's me." He beamed, his hands still shoved deeply in his pockets. "So about dinner?"

"Oh, yeah. You mentioned food, didn't you?"

"I know this great Poké place," he said, finally removing his hands from his pockets as he pointed in the direction Morgan assumed the restaurant was located.

"Sorry," she said. "I don't do fish," she lied, hoping she could get out of it altogether.

"Oh. That's okay. There's a deli over on Locust, and I always get the Wreck, which is fabulous."

"What's a Wreck?"

"Only the best sandwich ever. Grab your purse. We can get

some sandwiches and then maybe find a place for a couple of drinks after?"

Morgan hesitated. She didn't want to go. She had so much left to unpack, but dreaded the idea of declining. It would just be another uncomfortable interaction where she would end up feeling like an asshole.

"Give me just a moment," she said, leaving her door ajar as she walked to her kitchen for her keys.

When Morgan walked back around the corner and into her sitting area, Victor was standing next to her bookshelves, her decanter in his hands, pouring a glass of her whiskey.

"I hope you're not planning on driving," she said, causing him to jump.

"Oh. No." He chuckled. "I just figured you'd want to pre-game before we head out," he said, holding out her Glencairn toward her.

"Pre-game?" She lifted an eyebrow. "It's Tuesday and I have to work tomorrow."

"I'll just pour it back in," he said, as he tilted the glass.

"No! It's fine. One glass won't kill me." Morgan took it and then tossed back the contents of her rocks glass, sighing as the full taste hit her tastebuds.

"Ready to go?" Victor asked.

"As ready as I'll ever be." Morgan forced a smile as Victor placed his hand on the small of her back.

As they stood waiting for the elevator, Morgan felt unsteady. She leaned against the brick wall as she allowed it to hold her up. "Whoa." She blinked.

"You okay?" Victor asked.

"Yeah," she said, shaking her head. "Just a little warm."

"We can skip dinner if you don't feel well?"

"No. It's fine. I probably just need to eat. I can't remember what I've had today besides a couple of crackers and one... well, two glasses of whiskey." She shook her head.

"Your call?" he said, holding the elevator door open as she slowly stepped inside. "I figured we'd just walk to the deli, but maybe I should drive."

"Driving sounds good," she answered groggily.

The elevator doors closed, and her vision flashed in and out, sparks dancing before her eyes before strobing brightly when the metal ground harshly as the doors were forced back open.

Her ears pulsed with every heartbeat, a loud hum sounding off the elevator walls, and her mouth became incredibly dry.

"Morgan?" she heard her name called out from what seemed very far away. "Morgan?"

She tried to respond, then attempted to yell. She urged herself to move. *Just one step! One inch!* But something was wrong, and her legs didn't work.

Every message her brain sent went unanswered. Every desperate plea ignored. She was a prisoner, trapped in her own mind; forced to watch the world as it moved around her and she stood still.

The sound of mumbling—a voice, but not her own—was all she could discern as hundreds of electric like shocks assaulted her. Her palms tingled; an uncomfortable feeling that radiated to her fingertips as her ears filled with distant sounds: jingling keys and shoes clunking loudly as they hit the floor.

Clothes rustled as they were being removed, every thread scratching as it was tugged off her flesh. And she felt silken remnants on her back when her body fell back onto something soft, sinking in as she drowned in muddled thoughts.

Morgan then smelled cheap cologne and onions. Could feel hands groping and grasping, pulling at her as the air in the room seemed to swirl along the ceiling. And there he was—his face, abnormally large, as if she was still peering at him through the peephole.

He was so close. Too close with his hot breath invading her space and filling her nostrils while his tongue, that sandpapery, scratchy, unwelcome muscle traced her skin; pricking and piercing like barbed wire everywhere it lapped.

He was heavy, but it was more than just the weight of his body. It was the weight of the room as she was pinned down while her senses were assaulted. All of them. All at once. With no sign of reprieve.

There was just so much. It was just SO much. And just when she thought it would never relent, there was nothing.

Morgan was granted darkness. A nothingness. An escape of sorts. Some semblance of pity being taken upon her as everything washed away.

Morgan awoke the next morning with the sounds of a jackhammer in her head and a vague recollection of the previous day's events.

She recalled the debacle with the boxes, remembered arranging and unpacking the contents of her apartment, and had a vague memory of a neighbor—Victor, somebody or another.

Morgan sat upright in her bed, sliding her legs to its edge as she placed her feet on the floor.

That sudden change in attitude set her stomach on fire and she made a mad dash for the bathroom, closing the door as the contents of her stomach helped color the walls of her bathroom.

Great! I wasn't a fan of the color in here, but now I'll really have to do something about it, she thought as she struggled to gain her bearings.

Once she cleaned herself up, Morgan stomped heavily back to bed and crawled in, her feet brushing against something rough.

She drew her legs in and slowly reached her hand out, feeling the back of someone in bed next to her.

Oh, my God! You've got to be fucking joking me right now? I didn't think I'd had that much to drink and yet, there is some unnamed person in my bed. Wait, oh please God, no. Please don't let it be...

Just then, the body rolled over and Morgan was face to face with none other than her new neighbor.

What was his name? Dear God, why? Why do I get myself into these messes?

Morgan continued to chastise herself when he opened his eyes and said, "Hey."

"Hey," Morgan replied awkwardly.

"Last night was..." he trailed off as he ran his hands through his hair before propping his head on his hands behind him.

"Last night was nothing," Morgan said, getting out of bed with her sheet wrapped around her. "In fact..." she continued as she backed away toward her bathroom, "last night never happened. Deal?"

"What?" he answered, disappointed.

"These things happen," she said as she stood by the door. "Things that we didn't intend to happen. But they happen, and honestly... I'd just rather we forget the whole thing. And, if at all possible, never speak of it again. Now, please leave. I have to get ready for work."

Morgan went into her bathroom and locked the door behind her. She turned on the shower and listened closely for her front door to open and close.

When it finally did, she ran to the front door, quickly locking it once she was sure he was gone.

She looked through her peephole, watching as a back faded

away down the hall, and then bounced her head off her door as she cussed quietly, "Fuck. Fuck. Fuck."

Morgan waddled back to her bedroom, still swaddled in her sheet, and flung herself back on her mattress.

Immediately grossed out at the prospect of what happened in her bed, she stripped everything off, tossing it on the floor.

"You have got... to... be... fucking... kidding me!" she ranted as she kicked everything before her. "Ugh!"

She walked toward the bathroom and looked over at the mess she'd made: pillows and blankets and comforters tossed haphazardly in a heap at the foot of her bed.

Now in the bathroom, naked as she stood before the mirror, she wiped the steam off the surface and gasped.

As she stared, Morgan took notice of the bruises on the inside of her thighs and a very noticeable hickey on the right side of her neck.

"Fuck!" she strung out the word, yelling aloud as she stomped her feet.

CHAPTER 11

BUSINESS CASUAL

"Just my luck. It's fucking you again." Morgan sighed. "Don't you have a meeting of the trust fund babies to attend?"

Morgan had just walked in the door to the SSC Intimates' studio and was setting her bag down when Jamison walked in and looked around the space, stopping when his eyes landed on her.

"You just so happen to be in luck. They postponed that until next week, so I'm all yours. Well, all Alessandra's, anyway. The fact you're here, although a drawback, will not hamper my performance."

"Your performance?" Morgan chuckled aloud. "And what performance would that be?" she questioned as she brushed stray hairs away from her face, removing the hair tie securing her ponytail at her nape.

"Well, hopefully..." Alessandra interrupted, making her presence known, "his performance, and yours is hot as fuck. Otherwise, I am wasting not only my time but my money on you two," she announced in her sultry Mexican accent. She stepped forward

⚑ 121 ⚑

and kissed Jamison's cheek, and then Morgan's, in greeting. "Hello again, my lovelies."

"What do you mean 'on' us two?" Morgan asked her.

"You two seemed to know each other or I would have done the introductions. But seeing as you aren't picking up on the task at hand," Alessandra teased. "Señor Masters is your second."

"I'm no one's second anything," Jamison spoke up, offended.

"Primary. Secondary. Who gives a shit? It's all semantics. You two are shooting together today," she informed them, pointing at Jamison and then over at Morgan. "So get undressed, let wardrobe make you irresistible, and for the love of all that's holy... at least pretend like you want to fuck each other." She threw her hands in the air and walked off to take her seat next to the director.

As Jamison and Morgan were being poked and prodded by the stylists, having their hair and makeup done, and pulling off and on the different ensembles selected for their individual shoots, they just glared at one another, visibly irritated by the other's presence. But despite their obvious dislike of their selected partner for the day, they did not allow that to interfere with their performance and did their best to keep things professional.

Jamison was the first to shoot and walked onto the set wearing black distressed skinny jeans, a pair of thick heeled moto boots, and a fitted black button-down dress shirt with several of the top buttons left undone with the sleeve cuffs opened and rolled slightly up to his forearms.

They accessorized him with matching black leather O-ring wrist cuffs, choker, and a belt with twelve rings, one of which had a leather piece with two snap hooks on each end.

His hair was styled wet and tousled; a perfectly managed post coital look, while smudged and smoked out liner rimmed his eyes, and his already high cheekbones were accentuated with contour stick. Finally, they misted his face and neck to give him that glistening after sex glow.

The director positioned Jamison in the large picture window, having him lean back against the frame with one leg propped up, with his foot against the sill.

He tilted his head back against the window's edge and left his mouth open ever so slightly with lips pursed and accentuating his pout.

His dark hair, deep-set golden eyes, and the way he pushed his groin out as if someone was pulling him toward them by his belt, combined with the music blaring in the background, just screamed, *get over here and fuck me!*

He really is attractive, Morgan thought, appraising him.

Morgan's eyes lingered a little too long when they reached the bulge in Jamison's pants, his cock pulsing beneath his jeans as he shifted his stance.

He was getting turned on by this: by the attention and by the praise he received not only from the photographer but from Alessandra as well.

"Absofuckinglutely!" Alessandra cried out. "Pay attention, all of you. This is what I fucking want. I want chemistry. I want innuendo. I want passion. And for God's sake, I want it to make people want to fuck. I want it to feel good, like sex. I want it to feel like great sex. I want it to be raw, primitive, and lustful. But most of all… I want it to make people want to buy my shit." Alessandra laughed as she bit her thumb, looking lustfully at Jamison.

When it was time for them to get ready for their couples and group shots, Morgan finally attempted to make light of the situation and struck up a conversation with Jamison. "So, is this your first time doing this kind of thing?" she asked.

"Not exactly. Why? You?"

"This is the first time I've ever done anything like this professionally. But I am kind of natural in front of the camera." She smirked.

Stop it! You are not flirting with this asshole. No! she chastised herself.

Yes! You will flirt with this asshole... and you WILL play the part because Alessandra said this better be hot as fuck. Game face on, bitch. It's go time! she rallied.

"How do you feel?" Alessandra asked as she rubbed the backs of Morgan's arms calmingly.

"I feel..." Morgan paused, tilting her head to the side as she looked at herself in the full-length mirror. She trailed her index finger up the center line of the white corset she was wearing and rested her hand seductively at the base of her neck.

Looking Alessandra in the eyes where she stood staring back into Morgan's in the mirror behind her, she proclaimed, "I am sex. I am lust and longing. I am primitive and raw. And when people look at me wearing your designs... they'll not only want to buy your shit, but they'll also want to fuck me in it," she said, bending forward at the hip and pressing her ass out.

"That's my good girl," Alessandra cooed as she slapped Morgan's ass, turning and walking back to her chair. "Now you two..." Alessandra proclaimed, "show me just why I have chosen you, and that deciding to do things this way, as unorthodox as it is, was not a shit decision. Música! Let's go." She snapped her fingers.

"Do you mind if I pick it, Alessandra?" Morgan asked. "With the way the set is lit, and the choices the stylist made for this series, I have the perfect song to get me in the mood to deliver exactly what you're looking for."

"Por supuesto." She waved her hand toward Morgan before picking up her phone to record a clip as they shot the scene.

"Bueno." Morgan beamed, walking over to where the laptop that was bluetoothed to the speakers sat on top of the table on the other side of the room. All eyes were on her and the matching thong nestled in between her perfect ass cheeks as she sashayed effortlessly in the thigh-high, laced up six-inch strappy heels.

The sound of her heels clicking as she made her way across the room echoed as everyone waited in silence to hear her selection. She bent over, exaggerating her movements as she pushed her ass out.

"God damn!" The director hissed as he bit down on the knuckle of his index finger. "I take it back, Alessandra. All of it. I will never fucking question your decision again." He shook a finger in the air approvingly.

"I tried to tell you," Alessandra smiled, her eyes never leaving Morgan's silhouette. "Ella es perfecta."

Morgan walked seductively to where Jamison was restrained on the bed in the middle of the set as the first notes of the song "Daddy" by Ramsey vibrated the speakers.

Jamison's eyes widened when Morgan neared the edge of the bed and he glimpsed her ensemble for the first time.

What the fuck have I gotten myself into? he thought.

She grabbed his hand where it was fisted in the restraints, tightening the strap on one wrist before moving across the bed, leaning over him with her breasts brushing across his face while she grabbed and tightened the other.

Oh, I'm in fucking trouble!

"I do hope they aren't too tight, Mr. Masters," she cooed. "I'd hate to ruin this experience for you."

"You're already here," he said. "Can't get much worse."

Morgan threw her leg over his waist, drawing her face

extremely close to his, before she sat up and straddled him with her feet tucked underneath his thighs.

Then she reached down and fastened the leash in her hands to his choker, wrapping the ends around her palm twice before gripping it tightly. She leaned back with an exaggerated arch to her back and curve to her ass as she pressed her hips into him. She felt his body respond beneath her and heat shot straight to her core.

Oh, no you fucking don't! she thought, trying to calm her pussy down.

The director and photographer both called out, "That's it. Right fucking there. Hold that pose. Yes. Yes!"

Loving the praise, Morgan pulled Jamison up by the leash to a seated position, lording over him as she lifted his chin with two fingers, forcing him to look at her.

I can do this. I... can do this. I... nope, I can't do this, Jamison thought.

Morgan ran her thumb seductively across his lip before she leaned in and pulled it into her mouth. She bit down, tilting her head back slightly as she exaggerated the stretching of his flesh and the camera clicked successively, the flash sounding over and over as it whined each time it charged.

Jamison moaned quietly, his eyes tightly shut as his body reacted against his will. He wasn't sure who was in control—her or his body. Either way, this wasn't part of anything he'd pictured and he was struggling... hard.

Too hard. I'm too fucking hard.

Morgan rose to her feet, smiling triumphantly as she moved across the bed to release Jamison's hands from the restraints.

Once he was free, and still with a shit-eating grin on her face, Morgan clutched the leash in her hands, placing her heel on his shoulder. "Lick it!" she ordered.

Jamison followed her directions, grabbing her perfectly manicured foot and the heel that adorned it, pressing them to his lips. He then pulled her toes into his mouth, one by one, sucking each digit as his tongue swirled around them.

She groaned, pressing her heel into his chest and pushed him back on the bed.

The photographer continued to shower them both with praise. "You two are owning it. I'm getting hard just thinking about what you're going to do next."

The director cackled and then the photographer asked Alessandra, "It's okay I said that, right?"

"They don't mind. Do you?" Alessandra projected.

"Not at all," Jamison answered, his cock pulsing as he looked up at Morgan while she stood over him.

"Good. Now switch. I want some of him in the dominant posi-tion," Alessandra announced.

Jamison wasted no time, grabbing Morgan by the foot and ripping her legs out from under her. She fell backward onto her ass, and he quickly repositioned himself, kneeling facing her.

He grabbed her ankle and flipped her over, grabbing the back of her corset and pulling her up and into his chest. "My turn to ruin it," Jamison taunted, taking the leash out of Morgan's hands and tying its length around her wrists, binding them behind her.

Unclasping the leash from his choker, Jamison snapped it on the ties of Morgan's corset. He then trailed his fingertips up her arm, leaving goosebumps in their wake, as he slowly positioned his other hand at her throat.

He pulled her back against him, tightening his grip on her throat as her chin lifted and a gasp escaped her lips.

"Oh God," she whimpered, her eyes screwing shut as she fought to hold back her arousal.

"Yes!" Alessandra called out, standing on a chair as she recorded the scene from a different angle.

Jamison lowered his face, opened his mouth, and traced his tongue along Morgan's clavicle before raising his chin so he could bite down on her shoulder blade. She cried out as pleasure and pain washed over her.

Face first, he pushed her down into the mattress, leaving her ass in the air and on display for his eyes to feast upon.

"Boxers only! Take off your pants!" Alessandra cheered as she hopped up and down on her chair.

The photographer adjusted his position as Jamison stood, and wasting no time removing his jeans, he tossed them in a corner as the camera continued to click.

He returned to the set, taking up a position on his knees behind Morgan, and grabbed her wrists firmly as he positioned his groin tightly against her ass.

"Is that necessary?" Morgan grumbled from where her face was pressed into the mattress.

"We all have our parts to play. This just happens to be yours at the moment." He smiled triumphantly as he lifted her bound wrists skyward. "Feel free to cry out if it's too much."

Morgan and Jamison endured several hours of shooting where they got dressed, undressed, misted, and oiled up as they were transitioned from one set to the next. Each of them had taken turns binding and restraining the other, grinding and arching as they shifted from one position to the next, all while cheers and applause filled the air.

When it finally ended, Alessandra clapped loudly, showering everyone with praise as she thanked them for their efforts, and said she was certain her vision had been realized.

Morgan had just changed out of her last outfit when Alessandra walked over and handed it back to her. "Keep it. It's meant for you. You too," she said, motioning to Jamison. "In fact. I would be happy if you two could attend one of my events. Perhaps wearing my designs?"

"Any time." Jamison smiled coyly, buttoning his jeans as he looked to Morgan.

"Sounds good," Morgan replied, forcing a smile.

She shoved the outfit in her bag and was pulling her T-shirt over her head when Jamison walked over. "Ugh. What now? Wasn't that enough for you?"

"I just thought you might be hungry. Want to go grab something to eat?" he asked.

"Can't. I have a previous engagement." She pulled a strap over one shoulder, her bag hanging loosely at her side.

"After, then?" he asked, expectantly.

"It tends to go late. Maybe some other time." She pushed past him, walking out the door as his eyes followed her.

Alessandra walked over and stood next to Jamison, patting him on the shoulder. "Don't worry. She'll come around. She can try to deny it all she wants, but she was in every moment right along with you. None of what I saw today was an act. She's yours. She just doesn't know it yet," she assured him.

CHAPTER 12

THE AUDACITY

Morgan was sitting in her office when a text came in on her cell.

The callback list at the studio. As if your number is such a secret. I thought you plastered it on all the bathroom stalls for advertising purposes?

What TF is that supposed to mean?!

Let's just say that your 'extracurricular activities' are not as big of a secret as you think they are.

I have no idea what you're talking about.

Morgan lied, as infuriation overwhelmed her. She had worked so hard to avoid Jamison and not allow their feud to interfere with work, but this was the last straw.

It was bad enough she saw him all the time as she was entering or leaving her building. It was bad enough she had to endure that grotesque scene for Alessandra as the photographer and director cheered her on. But now he had her cell number to hurl his insults and pomposity at her at his leisure!

No. Fuck that. I've had about enough of this asshole!

Morgan stormed through the hallways of the hotel, looking for Jamison. This would end here. This would end now. And this would end today. Come hell or high water, she would have the last words. And Jamison? Well, he could only blame himself for the wrath he called forth because Typhoon Morgan was about to wipe his ass out.

Morgan rounded the corner and there Jamison stood with his hands in his pockets as he leaned against the bell cart, talking to Quentin while they waited for the elevator.

"Hey Morgan," Quentin greeted her.

Morgan iced Quentin out, her eyes not leaving Jamison for a moment as she seethed with anger.

The elevator doors opened and Quentin stepped inside. "See you downstairs, man?" Quentin asked warily.

"He'll only be a moment," Morgan said, forcing a smile as the elevator doors closed on Quentin, leaving Morgan and Jamison alone.

Jamison stood there smugly, looking at Morgan as he said, "Just couldn't let it go, could you? Had to have the last word."

"The last word?" she sneered. "I know you consider yourself to be very high on the horse, but around here, the deck is stacked in my favor."

"So it is a game, then—this back and forth? Hurling of insults and intentional agitations? You get off on it," he accused.

"No fucking chance in hell. There is nothing you could do that would ever get me off."

"Care to make a bet on that? Or do you only take a chance with your random hookups and whoremongers?" He took several steps forward, backing her into the wall as he closed the distance between them.

"Whoremongers? That's a nice way to talk about your friends," she said, pushing him back.

"Acquaintances are more like it. I am nothing like them. For example, I would not fuck you unless it was for sport."

"Someone's full of themselves. What makes you think I would ever fuck you for sport or otherwise?"

"It's simple, really. It would make for great content. And we know how you like to create content, don't we?" he sang.

"If you have something to say, just fucking say it."

"Does Alessandra know about your little side gig? I wonder how she would feel knowing her pride and joy is a whore for hire."

"And what exactly do you think it was that sold her on choosing me in the first place? It is a lifestyle she is selling, Mr. Masters, and I am exactly on brand. She wanted sex. I gave it to her. She wanted passion. I delivered. She wanted me to make people want to fuck, and now they do. She wanted people to buy her shit, and they very well have been. I have delivered on every promise she asked of me. What about you, Mr. Masters? What do you bring to the table?"

"Besides rock hard abs, a square jawline, and a big cock? What else does she really need from me? I'm not there to be poignant. I'm not there to speak. I am there to make you look more desirable. And as far as I'm concerned, I've delivered that shit in spades. You're very fucking welcome."

"I hope your mother didn't raise you to be a gentleman, because those words are anything but."

"And you are what now, a feminist? You're all feminists with your Chic Lit and your Indie music. You're all about being 'independent' until you're out on a date with a guy, then it's perfectly fine for them to pay for everything. So much for 50/50, huh?"

"I don't even know what the hell you're talking about, Jamison."

"Oh, Lucas told me all about it. He told me all about how he took you to dinner, he bought expensive food and wine, and then you guys went back to his place and you finally paid your half."

"Wow! I knew you were an asshole. I've seen your asshole tendencies. But you just keep outdoing yourself time and time again. So what's your damage? Caught your dad cheating on your mom?"

Jamison's mouth dropped open, and he just looked at Morgan, aghast.

"Ooh, and based on the look on your face, I'm not too far off. Oh wait, I know. Not only did you catch your dad cheating on your mom, but you and your mom both caught your dad cheating on your mom. And instead of being a strong 'independent' woman who can take care of herself, and getting out there and braving that big bad world on her own...," she mocked, "she stayed. So please... tell me how this anger, frustration, and animosity you have towards women, in fact, has absolutely nothing to do with your mommy issues, and everything to do with your daddy issues?"

Jamison took a step back.

"It seems I've struck a nerve," Morgan taunted.

"And you say I'm the asshole? Fine. My turn. You prance around here all prim and proper, but as soon as you walk out the front door, you suddenly morph into a street walker brandishing her wares for all to see. And when that doesn't pay enough, you take that ass to the inter-webs; on sale to the highest bidder. A dancing monkey waiting to turn the crank for the next person to place a coin in the tin. Well spread 'em pretty lady and tell me how all that is not about being left at the altar by some momma's boy who would've never made you happy in the first place."

A look of shock washed over Morgan as a single tear slid down her cheek.

"Now who's struck a nerve?" Jamison said as he walked away toward the stairwell and the fire escape. "Elevator's all yours."

CHAPTER 13

LIGHTS, CAMERA, ACTION!

"I stand corrected," Morgan muttered to herself as she rode the elevator downstairs. "He's no asshole. Jamison Masters has proven himself to be so much more than that. Jamison Masters is a prick," she spat, wiping the tears from her cheeks as she straightened her blouse before stepping out of the elevator onto the second floor.

As Morgan exited the elevator to the Mezzanine where she was meeting with the catering department to finalize the plans for that evening's social hour, she ran into Olivia.

"Morgan? What's the matter?" Olivia asked, grasping morgan by her arms.

"I don't have time to talk about it now." Morgan grimaced.

Olivia looked around and then pulled Morgan into the back hallway. As the doors closed behind them, Olivia asked, "Who the fuck did it and how badly do you want them dead?"

"Well, that depends, Olivia?" Morgan exaggerated her name. "Are you capable of digging your own grave?"

"Me?" she asked, her voice pitching up. "What did I do?"

"I did something with you I don't do. I trusted you!" Morgan raised her voice in anger. "I shared something with you in confidence. I shared the specifics about one of the most traumatic events of my life, only to have it thrown back in my face by none other than that asshole. Who, despite your better judgement and my warnings, you couldn't help but keep drooling over. So what was I?" Morgan questioned.

"Morgan, I don't understand?" Olivia announced, taken aback.

"Tell me how it happened?" she demanded. "Tell me exactly how Jamison Masters, of all people, came to know about Eric and I?"

Olivia's eyes widened as she realized just how badly she'd fucked up. "Morgan, I-."

"Save it!" Morgan interrupted her. "I just hope that gossiping about me over pillow talk was worth it because we are fucking done!" she seethed.

Morgan stormed out of the back hallway, slamming open the doors to the Mezzanine as her heels clicked loudly across the floor.

Olivia's eyes followed her friend, tears streaming down her cheeks as she slowly slid down the wall, the doors closing before her.

Just as Morgan was about to enter her meeting, she received an alert. She had a message from none other than Mr. Moneybags himself. He had been absent for some time now, so she needed to answer back. "Well, well, Mr. McDuck. To what do I owe the pleasure?" she said aloud.

Morgan ducked into one of the banquet rooms where she could open her site and reply in private.

His message read:

My little Vixen,

I am sorry I have deprived you of my company as of late. But rest assured, I have plans to make it up to you. I have a rather interesting proposition for you, but believe me when I say I want you to benefit solely from my generosity. Let's take this transaction externally, shall we? Look for a large pending transfer and we will discuss the details surrounding the arrangement for such? What do you say?

Just then, her phone dinged, alerting her to a very large transfer of $50,000.00 into her account.

She opened her gram messaging and responded, "You have my attention, sir. What do you have in mind?"

"I'm sending over a document via courier. It should be there shortly," he replied.

"Wait, what?" she exclaimed. *How the hell does he know where I work?*

Her walkie talkie buzzed, and Patrick at the front desk called out to her.

"Can I help you?" she asked.

"There's a delivery for the concierge," Patrick announced.

"I'll be right down."

Morgan walked into her meeting and informed them she would be back momentarily. She then took the elevator downstairs, walked past Jamison as she exited the lift, and arrived at the front desk where a courier was waiting.

"Package for Ms. Treble?" he asked, and she nodded in affirmation.

Jamison's ears perked up when he heard the name mentioned by the man in the foyer opposite the bell stand and listened in.

"Thank you," she said, accepting the envelope.

"Just sign here." The courier pointed.

Morgan signed, and the courier placed the clipboard in his backpack before exiting the hotel.

As Morgan turned to walk away, her phone buzzed with a

number she didn't recognize ringing in. Her caller ID labeled the incoming call from a S.W., P.C.

"Hello?" she answered. "This is. Whom may I ask is speaking? What can I do for you, Mr. White? Okay, fine then... Patrick. What can I do for you, Patrick? Yes, I have the document. Meet you? When? I can do five-thirty. Okay. No, I'll review it before then. Understood. See you then." Morgan hung up the phone and as she stood waiting for the elevator, she noticed Jamison glaring at her. "If you take a picture, it'll last longer." She sneered at him.

Morgan got sick of waiting for the elevator, so she took the back stairs to the second floor for her meeting.

Once Morgan was out of sight, Jamison excused himself to make a phone call in the back hallway.

"Hi, Mom. No, I'm good. Hey, quick question. What was the name of the lawyer dad uses here in town sometimes? No, I am not in any trouble. Call it genuine curiosity. Actually, I think one of my buddies works for him, is all. Yeah. Just wanted to see if it's the same guy. Patrick? Yeah, no. It's the same guy. Okay. Well, thanks Mom. Talk to you later. You too."

Jamison hung up the phone and cussed loudly. "Fuck! What in the hell is the old man up to now?"

He typed out a text to Kent to see if he could get to the bottom of it.

Jamison asked Kent to go through the files at the law office where he interned. He told him not to read any of the specifics, but that he wanted a copy of a certain document that was just delivered to a Ms. Treble. He didn't tell Kent the actual who or the why of the document he was requesting, but that it was important to him and of the utmost urgency.

> Look, dude. I would owe you so big on this one!

When Kent arrived an hour later, Jamison was on the verge of panic. He needed to sort this out before it was too late.

He hadn't known about Claire. He hadn't known about the "arrangement" she'd had with his father, and why he couldn't let her go. Hell, he didn't really want to let her go, but after a while, Marshall grew bored with her. He grew bored with her and their "arrangement" reached its end. So off she went, and on to greasing the pole of whatever CEO she saw fit to work for next. One thing's for certain, she ensured her job security. And sure as hell found her niche.

When Jamison saw the price tag that came with Claire's "services," it left him in shock. She had cost his father in one year more money than his Ivy league education had in all four of the years his father attended combined.

As Jamison read through the document, he just laughed.

"What?" Kent asked.

"Nothing man. It's just the sheer fucking gall."

"Do we know Nothing But Treble, LLC, and Baskerville Enterprises? Who the fuck is Carl Barks?"

"WE don't. But I do," Jamison said as he slammed the contract down. "Fuck!"

"Anything I can do, man?"

"No. We're good. Like I said, I owe you. Drinks tonight at my place?"

"Sure, man."

"And call Kentworth. Haven't seen his ass in person in a while and would love to toss a few back with him. He's got some stories you should hear. Shit will make you blush."

"Yeah?"

"Yeah, man. See you tonight," Jamison said as he walked into the back hallway and up to the break room to clock out.

[LIVE •]

Kent and Lucas showed up at Jamison's place at the lofts about nine that night. They bullshitted about school and summer plans, how Kent liked his internship, and if Jamison was enjoying his job at the hotel.

"Seriously, dude. Like, why the fuck are you even working there?" Kent asked. "It's not like you need the money."

"Call it genuine curiosity," he laughed.

"Curiosity about what? How much it fucking sucks to work?" Kent quipped.

"Something like that," he answered before taking another sip of his old-fashioned.

"And dude," Lucas chimed in. "Why can't you drink shots like the rest of us heathens? We get it, you're boujee. With all your high-end escorts and black-tie sex parties, how could you not be? But bring it back down to reality with the rest of us. Why don't you?"

"I'm boujee? Didn't you just take out some bitch and treat her to a thousand-dollar bottle of wine?"

"No fucking way?" Kent exclaimed. "Was she worth it, at least?"

"Worth it? Dude, she does this thing with her tongue. Swirls it under my dick as she takes it all in. And I mean ALL in," Lucas exaggerated.

"Tell him about your trip," Jamison pushed, his eyes twinkling with satisfaction. Getting those two together was just another element of his plan.

Lucas shared the details about his trip to Lincoln and the porn worthy fucking he delivered in the back of the truck.

"You're full of shit?" Kent announced, sinking back into the leather chair.

"Swear to fucking God, man. This chick is so DTF, and honestly, I dig it. She is one of a kind. She always smells like cherry vanilla," Lucas bragged.

"Yeah, well, I went on a first date and got a blow job in the coffee shop's bathroom we met at, not twenty minutes after we got there," Kent touted.

"Shut the fuck up, dude?" Lucas chuckled in disbelief. "You don't do hook ups. The only thing you know how to do is fall hard."

"So, is yours serious?" Kent asked Lucas.

"Is what serious?"

"The chick?"

"Nah, man. She's a casual thing. But I wouldn't mind several repeat performances. She does the cutest thing," Lucas mused.

"What?" Jamison asked.

"She giggles right after she orgasms."

"Stop." Jamison kicked Lucas' chair, leaning leisurely back as he looked over at Kent to see if he'd put the pieces together yet.

Still nothing. Huh? he thought.

"She does. It's adorable."

Whoomp! There it is, Jamison thought as realization washed over Kent.

Kent looked over at Lucas with his mouth agape. He slowly

slumped down in his chair before sitting up and grabbing another shot, slamming it down on the table between them all.

"Watch the furniture, man! What gives?" Jamison asked, feigning irritation.

"You realize we're fucking the same girl, right?" He threw the question out as an accusation at Lucas.

"Morgan? You're fucking Morgan?" Lucas sat with his mouth wide open.

"This shit just got interesting." Jamison smiled, leaning forward and bracing his elbows on his knees as he held back his cheers of triumph.

"Why?" Kent asked. "Are you fucking her too?"

"Nah, man. She works at the hotel with me and we had a photo shoot together, but that's it."

"Are you saying you wouldn't?" Kent asked.

"I mean…" Jamison trailed off, swishing his drink with an air of indifference.

"Geesh, man. You'd fuck anything," he accused.

"That's bullshit, man, and you know it. I am picky as shit."

"And yet, you'd fuck her," Lucas stated, irritated.

"You both just said she was a great fuck. You both think she's hot, so why is it a big deal if I would? It just proves we all have great taste." He held up his glass in toast, but when neither Kent nor Lucas met him over the table, he shrugged his shoulders and downed his drink.

"I thought you fucking hated her?" Lucas questioned, shocked.

"I am not a huge fan, no. But what does that have to do with fucking her? I don't have to like her to fuck her," Jamison offered.

"And that's where we differ," Kent said, shaking his head in protest. "I don't put my dick in chicks I don't like."

· · ·

They bantered back and forth about Morgan for the next thirty minutes, Kent and Lucas swapping the intimate details of their trysts and comparing notes, while Jamison brimmed with a sense of accomplishment.

As they were refreshing their drinks, Lucas and then Kent both got a text message from none other than "the Morgan Ericksson."

Silence filled Jamison's sitting room while the other two men read over their messages.

"Did you get the same shit I did?" Kent asked, handing Lucas his phone.

"Yeah," he said, scanning over the message. He scrolled up. "Oh, look. She sent you the same picture of her tits as she did me last night." Lucas looked over at Jamison. "She wants us to call her."

"Why are you looking at me? You don't need my fucking approval, Kentworth."

"Should I call her?" Kent asked.

"Do whatever the fuck you want," Jamison shrugged. "This is your drama. I'm just enjoying my popcorn from the cheap seats."

Lucas called Morgan first. He went out on Jamison's patio to the one place he could have some semblance of privacy.

"Hey, you," Morgan answered sweetly.

"What's up?" Lucas asked coldly.

Morgan wasted no time, skipping all the pleasantries and attempts to diffuse the awkwardness of the conversation with small talk, and went right to the gist of it.

"You want me to do what?" Lucas raised his voice.

"It's weird. I know. And I know you don't need the money, but will you at least consider it?"

He finished the call and then returned inside, where Jamison and Kent both looked at him as he entered, awaiting an update.

"You're up, kid. Don't keep her waiting," Lucas stated, taking another sip of his drink, and sliding his phone across the table.

Kent went outside and had relatively the same conversation as Lucas, returning inside afterwards. "Are we even considering this?" he asked Lucas.

"Are we considering what?" Jamison looked between the two with curiosity, despite already knowing the details.

Kent looked at Lucas and then over at Jamison before he busted out laughing. "Well fuck, man. It just so happens we need a third," he said, raising his glass to Jamison.

"So we're doing this, then?" Lucas asked.

"Might as fucking well. You don't need the money. But I, on the other hand, could do with an income. Not all of us have mommy and daddy's money."

Kent and Lucas finally filled Jamison in on not just what their messages had read but what Morgan relayed when they spoke. Then, one by one, Lucas and Kent messaged Morgan back to say they were in, not telling her they knew about her escapades with the other, or that they were together at the moment. Lucas told her he had a third in mind and to leave those details to him.

Morgan trusted Lucas and messaged back with a thumbs up emoji.

It would go down Friday night. There was a specified time slot: 9 p.m. to midnight. Three hours and they would each get ten thousand dollars, leaving the remaining twenty thousand for her.

⌜LIVE•⌟

Friday came, and all three men messaged back and forth throughout the day, joking about how they thought that night's events might transpire.

Kent and Jamison started the conversation:

> So, are you bringing your entire play closet, Masters? Or is the 'Dom Daddy' taking a break for the evening?

> Break? What's this break you speak of? 😌 It would be irresponsible of me to not take full advantage of this opportunity.

Lucas joined the group chat:

> And what makes you think Morgan will be up for your type of play, dude?

> Trust me. Miss Ericksson is more than accustomed to my brand and style of play.

> If three weren't a requirement for this contractual endeavor, I highly doubt she would let you through her door with your playthings.

> Oh, she'll be down for my playthings. Hell, you two might even be down for my playthings.

Lucas replied nervously:

> What's that supposed to mean?

What I am saying, my dear Kentworth, is that you have never known pleasure like tying a woman up and making her scream out your name because you were able to deliver her pleasure from way more than just your dick! 😈 Driving her to the edge, teasing and provoking her, making her so aroused she raises her hips to meet you, as her body just begs you to dominate her…

Kent chimed in after staying silent for several minutes:

Yeah, and you've done that, have you?

Oh, I have done that. I have fucking mastered it. It's like you said, Adams. I'm the Dom Daddy, and I will make her submit to me before the three hours are up. She might even beg me for another scene once the clock strikes twelve. Cinderella will be bound and gagging on my cock, unable to flee the ball. She won't hear a damn sound as the clock tolls midnight because the only striking she'll hear is my balls against her ass.

Lucas chimed back in:

Just wait Kent. He's talking a good game now, but come time to deliver, how much you want to bet this asshole can't even get it up? Hard to make her legs shake and body quiver when you're gripping tightly to a limp noodle begging him to come to life. It'll be a lot less Cinderella and more like Pinocchio wishing he was a real boy! LMFAO

Laugh all you want now, man. You two make her giggle when she comes, but I am determined to make her fucking scream.

⌈LIVE•⌋

The two men met at Jamison's place at 8:00 p.m. and started pre-gaming with a few shots of bourbon, throwing in a mixed drink or two to calm their nerves. No one had ever been asked to perform for an audience before, except Jamison, so they were nervous.

Jamison had recorded his play sessions and "sexcapades" frequently. His brand of porn was homemade, and nothing says vanity like getting hard to yourself, giving it to some chick with the camera rolling.

"Last chance to bow out gracefully, Masters," Lucas teased.

"Not a chance, man. I'm locked, cocked, and ready to rock," he boasted as he grabbed his dick through his dress pants.

"I feel like we are filming an actual movie," Kent laughed nervously as he struggled to tie his necktie.

The three men dressed almost identically, save the color of their button up shirts. Lucas wore charcoal, Kent black, and Jamison an almost burgundy. They all had on dress slacks, pointed-toed suede loafers, leather belts, cuff links, neckties, and had blazers on the back of their chairs.

"Stop!" Lucas commanded. "Watching you fumble fuck tying a Windsor knot is torture. Let me do it."

Lucas stepped up behind Kent, reaching around him and grabbing hold of the necktie. He was standing very close, his cock brushing lightly against the back of Kent's ass as he continued securing the knot.

"There," Lucas said, placing both his hands on Kent's shoulders. "Some lawyer you'll be if you can't tie a tie, dude," Lucas teased, whisking a kiss across Kent's cheek.

A look crossed Kent's face and Lucas immediately felt awkward, stepping away from him as he reached back and smacked his ass. "Good game!"

"Dumbass," Kent mused, still unsure of what had transpired just then.

"You two quit playing grab ass and let's go," Jamison ordered.

"Alright. Alright. Someone's antsy to get his dick wet," Kent jeered.

They left the penthouse and took the elevator down the several floors to Morgan's. Lucas stood in front, knocking as Kent and then Jamison stood after him, one directly behind the other.

Morgan called out for them to enter and, one by one, they entered the loft like a group of inmates being brought in for a lineup: heads down, feet shuffling anxiously forward, and then coming to a stop without lifting their heads to make eye contact.

"Don't look so fucking excited to be here," she teased as she tightened the laces on her corset. "Looks like a fucking funeral procession. I swear to you, no one is gonna die from having sex on camera. Trust me."

She looked at Lucas, Kent, and then finally her eyes landed on Jamison, who stood somewhat awkwardly at the end of the line with a rolling duffle bag. "Absolutely fucking not! No. Not him. Why did you have to bring him?" Morgan pouted as she rolled her eyes and walked away. "I'm going to need another drink."

"Don't be so bitchy. You act like this is my idea of a good time. I told you I would only fuck you for sport. And now, here we are." He grinned.

"You are enjoying this a little too fucking much," she chastised.

"Yeah, well. I will probably say the same about you shortly."

Morgan pointed to Lucas and Kent, her jaw clenching before she said, "This better work. If this doesn't go smoothly..." she trailed off.

"Relax, Morgs," Lucas said, walking up behind her and rubbing her shoulders.

"Please don't call me that," she frowned, shrugging him away. "Anything else. Just not that." Morgan tossed back the rest of her drink, rolling her neck as Lucas went back to rubbing her shoulders.

"Game faces on," Kent said, his feet shifting as he swayed.

"You alright, Adams?" Jamison asked. "You look a little green."

"I'll be okay once we get going. It's just a little anxiety. Honestly, I don't get how you all are so damn calm."

"Because I know I am an excellent fuck, Jamison is a Dungeon Daddy, and Morgan, apparently, is a professional. Which, come to think of it, explains a lot."

"Hey!" Morgan raised her voice in offense.

"It's not a judgement. I am beyond happy with how things turned out."

"Still." She glowered at him.

"Look, I never saw something like this in our cards. But honestly, chasing this dopamine has been amazing. More of a rush than racing," Lucas admitted.

"And if I do my job right..." Morgan grinned, stepping toward Lucas and running her hands over the lapel of his blazer, "much more satisfying of a ride."

"Quite." Lucas smiled.

"Quit stroking each other's ego and let's go over the specifics," Jamison pushed.

The trio sat in Morgan's sitting area, discussing not necessarily a storyline but the order of introduction of each man and what they imagined for their scene with her.

Jamison sat silently, listening in as Lucas, Kent, and Morgan outlined the specifics of the contract itself.

"So the basics are, you as the primary and sole focus of the filming, yes?" Lucas asked.

"Yes," Morgan agreed.

"And then, three hours is the time constraints under which we are operating?"

"Uh-huh." She nodded.

"So what does this Mr. Moneybags expect to see in those three hours?" Kent questioned.

"Key elements are self-play. That's all me. Undressing of the businessmen, and as their secretary, seeing to their needs. That's you." She pointed at Kent and Lucas. "And then individual scenes with me and each man, as well as group scenes with two, and eventually three male partners, culminating in a group scene with all three engaged in the scene with me."

"So, how many holes are we talking about here?" Jamison wisecracked.

"Dude?" Lucas looked at Jamison with his mouth agape.

"What? Don't you need to know which holes are a go or a no-go?"

"I figured she would fill us in when it comes to it," Lucas said.

"That's not how scenes work, dude. Everything gets discussed and agreed upon prior to. No time to ask questions if you're about to go nut to butt."

"Come on?" Kent winced, looking away in shock.

"Morgan?" Jamison said, gesturing to her. "Am I wrong about any of this?"

She just smiled and let out a loud chuckle.

"What?" Jamison asked.

"I've never heard nut to butt before, is all." She smiled at Jamison for once.

"Well, I have no intentions of going nut to butt," Kent said, placing his hands on his hips.

"Oh, I'm going to put whatever she lets me wherever she wants it." Lucas laughed.

"It's not funny!" Kent looked on wide-eyed.

"Kent, I fucked you in the bathroom of a coffee shop and you are getting worked up about a little ass play?" Morgan quipped.

"No. I just want to make sure that nothing is going near mine, is all."

"Oh my God! Relax, asshole. I'm not looking to fuck you," Lucas assured Kent.

"Good." Kent relaxed a bit.

"What about me? Do you have plans to fuck me?" Jamison asked.

"I didn't plan on it. Why? Do you want me to fuck you?" Lucas raised a brow.

"I hadn't really thought about it. It's not off the table." Jamison shrugged.

"That's not how scenes work, dude. Everything gets discussed and agreed upon, prior to," Morgan teased, as she made fun of Jamison.

"Fuck off, Morgan."

"No. Fuck you, Jamison. Or perhaps I'll just leave that to Lucas." She cheesed.

"You can't be serious?" Kent squirmed.

"If you can't handle this, I can always call up Victor. He's been dying to fuck me again."

"Again?" Jamison questioned.

"Long story. One I'd rather not revisit."

Morgan continued to move things around in her sitting area, setting up her equipment with her bed in the center of the room. It had the makings of a professional porn set, with lighting and multiple cameras set up for the different angles, and staging areas for people and props off camera and out of view.

Jamison was using Morgan's coffee table to set out all his toys. He was meticulous in his preparation and display.

"Seriously, dude?" Kent asked Jamison, looking on as he spaced out his plugs in increasing sizes with two finger separations between them.

"What? Man, this is an art-form. You don't have to get it. But just know the anticipation she will have seeing me walk to my treasure trove, trying to figure out which goodies I'm going to use on her and when is just part of the buildup. She will tense and relax, sometimes hold her breath in anticipation," he said as he caressed his dragontail longingly. "It just adds to it all. You get it, don't you?" Jamison asked, looking over at Morgan as he pulled out his Fluffinator—a black and burgundy, faux fur tasseled instrument of enjoyment.

It was deceitfully decadent, and he placed it right beside its matching fluffy flogger. They looked identical and she would not know which tasty treat she would get until it finally made contact.

Morgan's eyes widened as she looked at the items placed before her. "Is this the order you plan to use them?" she asked.

"Tsk, tsk, tsk," Jamison taunted. "Telling you my methods will ruin all the fun of it. The best part is you not knowing which comes next."

"You are enjoying this a little too much." She smirked.

"I am. Oh, I really am." Jamison continued to set out his trinkets while Kent just walked away.

"I'm going to the bathroom really quick," Kent stated.

"Hurry," Morgan instructed. "You're on in fifteen."

"Okay, task master. I got it." He mock saluted.

In the bathroom, Kent splashed water on his face, looking at himself in the mirror as he quietly hyped himself up. "You can do this. You... can do this. You've been having sex for years. This is nothing new. Come on man," he said, looking down at himself. "Do or die. Don't fail me now."

"Stop talking to your dick and get out here!" Lucas shouted, pounding on the door.

"Fuck off, dude!" Kent challenged through the door.

Kent walked out of the bathroom, a visible erection trapped behind his slacks, and smiled as he flipped Lucas off.

Morgan chuckled and said, "Guess that means you're up first."

"Sloppy seconds isn't really my jam," Kent mused.

"Jam, jelly, seconds or thirds, I don't give a shit." Lucas grinned. "I'll take it all."

"Yes, you will," Jamison teased, smacking Lucas on the ass.

"Stop with all the gay shit before I lose my hard on." Kent grimaced.

"Kent says that now, but just wait until he has my balls resting on his chin as he gags on my beautiful cock." Jamison beamed.

"Not happening," Kent assured him.

"You say that now," Lucas added. "Let's see what happens once we get going."

Morgan turned on her sound system and linked it to her laptop, selecting her favorite song, "Who Do You Want" by Ex Habit, to start the scene.

"A little mood music to get the juices flowing."

"That's my job," Kent said, sauntering up behind Morgan as he pressed his dick against her ass.

"While I appreciate your enthusiasm," Morgan said, reaching behind her as she gripped him through his slacks.

"Let's save it for on camera." Morgan tapped him gently before walking away.

"Fucking tease." Kent growled.

"Dude, you are about to be balls deep in her pussy as some dude watches. There is no teasing to it." Lucas chuckled.

Morgan centered herself on the bed, her long legs extended out with lace up, dark red leather and ribbon high heels criss-crossing her calves. She had on a black laser-cut masquerade mask, a burgundy silk robe, and coordinating lace corset and panties.

The color of the fabric accentuated her natural golden hue, making her amber-colored eyes pop behind her lush lashes. She was a vision in crimson. A seductive siren beckoning Kent forth as she caressed herself over the softness of the fabric.

"Are we rolling already?" Lucas whispered in Jamison's ear as they stood off camera, each of them tying their coordinating masks behind their head.

"9:02 p.m." Jamison lifted his Rolex to show Lucas.

Morgan started the self-pleasure scene, ignoring the others in the room. Her hands meandered along every curve, shifting the silk across her skin as her fingertips traced the line of her hip, before swooping down to caress her lips through the crotch of her panties.

Her head fell back, and she arched, lifting her hips as she gyrated to the music. Her movements were fluid and seductive, choreographed to allow for the utmost enjoyment of the watcher.

Who was this watcher? Kent wondered as he salivated, the anticipation of his entrance into the scene building.

Kent watched as Morgan slid one, then two fingers under the band of her garments, collecting the moisture that pooled there. She drew her fingertips up her body before placing them at her lips. She gasped, her tongue caressing as it licked her juices from her digits.

She arched her back once again, extending her toes toward the camera, giving the viewer an amazing view of the inside of her thighs, straight to the sweet spot.

She began gliding her lace panties down her legs, stopping with them at the crook of her knees as she lifted her legs straight in the air. She slid her hands down to her ass. It was an incredible sight: smooth, perky ass, inviting lips, and just the right amount of honey dripping between her creases.

With her legs still in the air, Morgan motioned with her fingers, beckoning Kent to join the scene.

He entered the frame and slowly removed his blazer, and loosened and removed his tie before discarding his shirt. He stood staring down as Morgan played with her pussy, his muscular back facing the camera.

"All that fucking work on that tie, and for what?" Lucas whispered to Jamison.

Kent slowly crept across the bed, sliding her panties the remainder of the way off, and tossed them away before taking up residence between her thighs. He looked up at her expectantly.

Morgan grasped the back of Kent's head, urging him forward and welcoming him to savor her.

As the intoxicating scent of her arousal invaded his nostrils, Kent gave in to his desires. His trepidation washed away as he buried his face in her.

Kent traced Morgan's opening, pulling every ounce of her expectation into his mouth where it danced across his tongue. Explosions of that sweet, sticky satisfaction twirled on the tip of his tongue as he darted in and out of her.

Morgan's body reacted to every movement from Kent, and when he slid one finger inside of her, his tongue not slowing the tempo at all, she cried out. Her cries of pleasure egged him on, propelling his need into overdrive.

He sucked greedily on her clit, sending her spinning as she glazed his chin. He did not withdraw. He continued his attack on her nether regions, drawing her to the edge before throwing her right over as she melted beneath him.

He needed to be in her. He needed to feel her mouth on his cock. Needed her to deliver that sensation only she could.

Kent moved to the head of the bed, positioning himself above Morgan as she looked up at him from where her head hung off the edge. He unfastened his pants and slid down his zipper, pulling his cock out for her.

She reached up and took hold of him, cupping his balls as she said, "Is all this for me?"

"You can have as much as you want," Kent offered.

She licked her lips and let out a moan of gratitude before she traced the head of his dick across her lips. He watched as she played with him, kissing his tip before twisting that torturous tongue across his opening.

His head fell back, and a moan escaped him. That first sign of ecstasy; that was Lucas' cue to join in.

Lucas slowly entered the scene, looking over at Kent, who cradled Morgan's head in his hands, guiding himself in and out of her mouth as she pulled him into the back of her throat.

She gagged a little, as her airway closed off from time to time, the deeper he thrust.

Lucas wasted no time removing his blazer, tie, and shirt before crawling up and burying his face between Morgan's thighs, lapping up the flavor his tongue had been antsy for.

He rubbed the tip of his nose up, down, and around her clit, kissing back and forth across her lips before biting playfully at the softness of her inner thigh.

She pulled back slightly with the sensation, but then settled as Lucas continued his worship of her.

Off camera, Jamison watched as Morgan gave and received pleasure from both of his friends, massaging his erection over his slacks.

How did I not realize how incredibly skilled she was before now? How did I not know how good at this she would be? he thought.

Morgan was full of surprises, and Jamison's anticipation climbed to a fever pitch as he waited for the time when he, too, could satiate his need within her.

Jamison had fantasized about such a scene. He had imagined fucking her senseless, all his toys in play as his dad was forced to watch. Taking liberties with her as the 'old man' sat helpless to stop him; only able to watch as he enjoyed what his father hoped to claim as his own.

He couldn't wait. He couldn't resist the intrusive thought that popped into his head. Jamison decided he would take this thing somewhat off script when it was his turn. A final fuck you to good ole Marshall before the time elapsed.

Lucas inched forward, moving within reach so Morgan could unfasten his slacks as he straddled her chest.

She massaged him through his pants before she undid them. He slithered back down her body and slid his pants the rest of the way down.

Once he was free of his slacks, Lucas slowly entered Morgan, holding her ass in his hands as he pressed forward. She enveloped him, her velvety center drawing him deeper as he clenched his cheeks with each forward pulse.

His pace increased, and as it did, so too did her body's response. She lifted her hips to meet him, drawing him deeper and deeper each time. They had created a rhythm; Lucas fucking her upward as Kent thrust forward and her body bouncing in between them.

The corset trapped Morgan's breasts, and Lucas wanted to see them moving along with their rhythm, so he reached forward and carefully released one breast after the other from where they were constricted by boning and ties.

It was a beautiful sight, the accordion-esque movement of all three as they came together in sequence, and Jamison gave in to temptation, putting his hands down his pants as he watched on in fascination.

Their dance continued for a time before Jamison removed his hand from his pants and walked over to his cache of playthings, grabbing a red leather collar from the table. He nonchalantly walked onto the scene, not interrupting the movements of the three, and stood looking down at them all.

They stopped momentarily to look over at him. Once they did, Jamison reached down and fastened the collar around Morgan's neck, walking back over to his collection and grabbing the matching leash.

Jamison re-entered the scene, handing the end of the leash to Kent after fastening it to Morgan's collar. "Continue," he instructed. "I'll just be over here planning my grand entrance." He smirked.

The three changed position, flipping Morgan over onto her knees.

"My turn," Kent said, handing Lucas the leash. "Switch."

"High five, rotate." Lucas chuckled as he moved around the bed, standing before Morgan's head.

Kent slid his pants down before kneeling on the bed and positioning himself behind her.

Morgan was on all fours, her beautiful ass tilted upward

toward Kent as Lucas gripped tightly to the leash, pulling her head forward toward him.

"Care to do the honors?" Lucas teased, gripping his dick before Morgan.

She opened her mouth wide, dropping her jaw as he slid his cock into her.

Lucas wrapped the leash in his palm, placing his hand at the back of her head so he could direct his dick in and out of her mouth. "That's my fucking good girl," he praised. "Take it all." He thrust forward, leaning his head back and enjoying every caress of her skilled tongue as it zig-zagged along his shaft.

Jamison once again entered the scene, bringing a plug to Kent after he lubricated it liberally, dropping the tube on the bed. "Here," he said, handing it out to Kent, who paused.

"What am I supposed to do with this?" Kent asked.

"Oh, my young Padawan," Jamison teased, wiggling the plug back and forth. "Watch and learn. Spread her cheeks apart," he directed.

Tapping Morgan's hip, Jamison gained her attention.

She stopped and turned to look back at Jamison who mouthed quietly, "Did you prep?" Her eyes sparkled, and she smiled, nodding quickly before turning her attention back to Lucas.

With Morgan's acknowledgement and Jamison's instruction, Kent spread Morgan's ass cheeks apart. Lucas halted his movements as he watched Jamison position the plug at Morgan's opening, slowly adding pressure and sliding the toy in place.

"Why does it have a gem on the end?" Kent asked quietly, once the plug was in place.

"Girls like pretty things," Jamison said as he patted Kent on the shoulder before exiting the scene. Kent's eyes followed Jamison as he walked off set. "Well, go on now, man. Don't leave her waiting. She's all dressed up and you're leaving her with nowhere to go." He waved his hands and Kent turned his attention back to Morgan and the scene.

"No going back now, I guess," Kent said as he slowly slid his dick into Morgan's pussy. "Oh, God damn," he called out.

"You're welcome." Jamison laughed as he stood leaning against Morgan's bookshelf with his arms crossing his chest. He was done teasing himself as he watched. He intended to save himself for his finale.

The scene continued, Lucas and Kent taking turns as they moved Morgan into varying positions while Jamison offered and removed toys from the play area. And now the coffee table was full of items needing a good soaking after the session was over.

With thirty minutes left on the clock, Jamison finally joined in on the play. He had never been with Morgan before, and wasn't sure how much she could take, so he handed the nipple clamps to Lucas, who affixed them to Morgan. She drew in a breath and Lucas' cock popped out of her mouth when she did.

"How are you doing?" Jamison asked her.

"I'm good." She sighed, still on all fours, with Kent behind her and Lucas standing still before her as she looked back at Jamison.

"Okay. Still good with the plug, or are you ready for me?" he asked.

"Either, or," she said.

Jamison stepped toward the head of the bed, everyone halting as they watched him undress.

Morgan had her head down as she waited, and Jamison walked to her side.

"Call me selfish, but I'm feeling the need to experience you myself," he said, gripping her jaw as he forced her to look into his eyes. He leaned over and kissed her hard, biting down on her lip as he pulled back. "Let's go, man. Slowly grab hold of that gem you like so much and ease it out. Gently," Jamison insisted, pointing back at Kent as he walked toward the end of the bed.

Kent did as he was told and once he was done, dropped the plug onto the bed, his eyes wide with the overstimulation of it all.

"Are you okay?" Jamison asked, standing beside him. "You're a little flushed."

"It's a lot. But it's fucking fabulous," Kent admitted. Kent reached over and grabbed Jamison, pulling him down to his face, where he kissed him.

"I fucking told you!" Lucas clapped from where he stood at the head of the bed in front of Morgan, who looked back over her shoulder, smiling. "Now it's a party." He slapped the bed.

Jamison gripped Kent's face in his hand. Glaring at him, he sneered. "You didn't ask. I'm going to make you pay for not asking permission." He pushed Kent's face away. "But don't worry, you'll like it."

Jamison walked back to all his playthings and grabbed his Fluffinator and another collar: black leather with a matching leash. He attached the leash to the collar and fastened the collar around Kent's neck, retaining the leash in his hand with the handle of the Fluffinator.

Stepping onto the bed, Jamison straddled over Morgan, who was still on all fours with Lucas' dick back in her mouth while Kent was nestled happily in her pussy, her ass sans the plug. He unfastened his pants, pulling his cock free as he stood lording over Kent.

"Open," Jamison commanded.

Kent opened his mouth, the fear evident in his eyes as he looked up at Jamison.

"Relax, man. I won't make you gag on it," he said as he placed his hand under his chin. "This time." He smirked as he pinched Kent's face in his hand. He slid his cock over Kent's pouty lips.

"Don't move," Jamison insisted, clutching the leash in his palm. "I'll move how I want. You just keep that mouth of yours open."

Kent attempted to answer and Jamison delivered a blow from the Fluffinator across his back. Kent winced, arching his back slightly, and the garbled sound he made vibrated Jamison's cock.

"No talking with your mouth full," Jamison scolded, tugging up on the leash. "That's strike one. Keep that shit up and I will be punishing your ass instead of riding Morgan, understand?" Kent blinked his eyes once in response to Jamison. "Better."

Lucas chuckled from where he was positioned in front of Morgan. He and Morgan had stopped their movements to watch what was unfolding between Jamison and Kent.

Jamison looked over his shoulder at Lucas as he continued to thrust forward into Kent's mouth. "What are you laughing about? Keep it up and I'll punish you next."

"Don't threaten me with a good time," Lucas teased, smiling.

Jamison pulled his cock out of Kent's mouth and pushed him back away from Morgan, forcing him to withdraw from her.

"My turn," Jamison insisted, guiding Kent around the bed with the leash. "Matter of fact..." Jamison trailed off. "Everyone, stop and let's shift positioning. You on your back." He pointed at Lucas. "You riding him." He tapped Morgan. "I'll take command from back here for a little double penetration, and you will get the honor of standing before me. Deal?"

They all agreed and moved into position.

Morgan straddled Lucas, sliding slowly down the length of his cock before she leaned forward onto his chest. Jamison moved forward, coating his dick with the lube that he tossed back on the bed before placing his head at her opening, sliding forward slowly. She tensed around him. Jamison had Kent hand him Morgan's leash, that he wrapped around one hand as he gripped the side of her hip, and Kent stood in front of him, straddling the entire group. Jamison reached for Kent's leash, wrapping it in his other hand before grabbing Morgan's other hip with it.

Once they were all set, Kent slid his cock into Jamison's mouth, closing his eyes tightly as he leaned his head back. They all synchronized their movements, moving as one entity as their passions built.

The room was filled with a distinctive sex smell. It was a combination of sweat, bodily fluids, and Morgan's cherry vanilla lotion.

Morgan cried out loudly as the feeling of Jamison and Lucas' movements overwhelmed her. They touched and stretched every inch of her, sending a feeling of fire flicking its tongue as it licked across every inch of her body while her nerves responded to it all.

She was about to crest. She was about to break and their time was almost at an end. She didn't want it to stop. She didn't want them to stop. She needed and wanted them all.

Morgan called out for Kent, pleaded for him. She wanted him in her mouth so that every hole was filled when she came.

Jamison released his control of Kent and allowed him to move in front of Morgan, where she pulled his beautiful, saliva coated cock into her mouth.

She could taste the remnants of Jamison's saliva. It had a bourbon aftertaste, smoky and sweet with hints of vanilla.

Kent was close and on the edge of explosion. Jamison had brought him there, but Morgan was going to push him over the fucking edge. He could feel himself tense, his tip so sensitive he was teetering on the precipice as Morgan's throat constricted around him. "I'm going to cum!" he cried out.

"Me too," Jamison announced.

"Might as well," Lucas offered, a strained quip.

Just as Jamison was about to climax, he tore off his mask and looked straight into the side view camera. This was how he'd planned it. This was what he'd envisioned in his mind. *Fuck you, old man,* he thought.

"She's fucking mine now, old man!" he shouted, spilling every ounce of himself into Morgan, pulsing forward several times until he stilled.

With his cock still buried deep inside her, Jamison's chest heaved and his breaths came hurriedly.

The live stream ended, the laptop dinging as the session expired, and someone's phone alarm sounded from across the room. That was it. It was over. They were done. And now his father would know that he knew. About Morgan... and about him.

CHAPTER 14

ALL'S WELL THAT ENDS WELL

"Hello, son," Marshall called out from where he was leaning against the side of his silver Range Rover, just outside the entrance to the lofts.

"Dad? What are you doing here?" Jamison said through gritted teeth.

"I could ask you the same thing," Marshall accused.

Just then, Morgan walked out of the building and stopped, looking back and forth from Jamison to his father, and then back again.

"I think I'll just get a coffee before work. Later, Jamison." Morgan walked away briskly, after obviously interrupting something.

"Well, that explains at least one thing," his father acknowledged.

"Why are you here, Mr. Masters? Don't you have places to be and people to screw over?" he exaggerated.

"This is no time for jokes, seeing as I am not the one who is screwing people over," Marshall spat.

"What the hell are you talking about?"

"I saw you," his father gritted.

"You saw me, what?" Jamison smiled.

"I saw you and that girl!" He pointed after Morgan. "I saw you and your loser friends," he said, squeezing the bridge of his nose where the pressure grew as a migraine sprung forth.

"Careful, Marshall. You'll undo all that Botox. And we all know how you hate to waste money."

"You think this is funny? You think this is a fucking joke?" Marshall said, stepping forward and grabbing Jamison by the back of the arm and digging his nails into his flesh. "I saw everything. My colleagues saw everything!"

"Get your fucking hands off me!" Jamison jerked his arm away and stepped further from his father.

"Do you have any idea what you have done to me? Do you have any idea what this will do to your mother? The damage you have caused?"

"The damage I have caused?" Jamison yelled. "What about all the damage you have caused? And somehow you're worried about how I behave might affect my mother? What about the damage you have caused my mother?"

"Your mother... has forgiven me for my past indiscretions and we are working on moving past it. But this... this stunt of yours is reckless. Sheer stupidity. And it jeopardizes everything."

"For whom? I stand unaffected. Or can't you tell?"

"Actions have consequences, Jamison. Even though I know you are just doing this to punish me." Marshall winced.

"Not every fucking thing is about you, dad!" he exaggerated. "Maybe I liked it. Maybe it filled a void I didn't know I had. Maybe it presents an opportunity for me to make something of myself outside of the path you have chosen. Did you ever think of that?"

"So your plans are what now, to become a porn star? Fucking your way to the top of a widely saturated food chain?"

"Nah, Dad. I'll leave the fucking their way to the top to you."

Marshall reacted before he could stop himself. He reared back and back handed Jamison, sending spittle flying.

Jamison reached up and rubbed his jaw where his father had just delivered a shocking blow. "We're fucking done." Jamison sneered, walking around his father and across the street.

"This isn't over!" Marshall yelled after him.

Jamison ignored his father as he called after him. He got into his vehicle, speeding off through downtown.

He's got some fucking nerve! Coming here and lecturing me about making smart choices and how my actions have consequences. When do his actions have consequences? When does he have to pay for his shit behavior?

Just then, an incoming call rang through the speakers, and he pressed the phone button on the left side of his steering wheel. "Mom?"

"Are you going to tell me what happened?" she asked.

"Nothing to say."

"Then why has your father called me and asked for me to get a handle on 'my son'?"

"It's nothing. And I fucking love how when he wants me to do something, and I have somehow fucked up in his eyes, he calls you and says that you need to get a handle on 'your' son. As if my shortcomings can in no way be a product of him? Or that my reaction could in no way relate to anything he'd done?"

"Okay. Okay, I'll deal with your father. Just give me some time," Melody promised.

⌈LIVE •⌋

"Jamison Elijah Masters!" Melody screeched as she entered the break room at the hotel later that morning. She stood in the doorway, crossing her arms in disapproval.

"Mom? What are you doing here?" Jamison asked, his cheeks flushing with embarrassment.

Jamison and Morgan had been standing in the break room enjoying their mid-morning coffee when Melody Masters, Jamison's mother, walked in.

"Apparently, if your father is to be believed, I need to be asking you the same thing. What the hell is it you think YOU are doing?"

"I think I'll show myself out," Morgan muttered nervously, walking toward the door where Melody stood.

"I don't know where you think you're going, young lady. This involves you just as much as it does him. A mask may have hidden your face, but I know you're behind this stupidity."

"I'm sorry?" Morgan choked on the words as they escaped her lips. "How do you figure?"

"Well, seeing as you have taken it upon yourself to corrupt my son into participating in this nonsense of yours; it has everything to do with you," she chastised.

"No offense, Mrs. Masters, but I already have a mother. So you can spare me your judgement and indignation. And another thing…" Morgan turned around before walking out the door, "I'll not be shamed by you or anyone else. Reality check, it's just sex."

"It's never just sex. You'll understand that when you're older."

"Your son and I barely tolerate one another, and I wouldn't necessarily even say that we like each other," Morgan admitted. "So yeah, it was just sex."

"Yes, well. All of that was clear during that little performance of yours."

"You watched it?" Jamison accused. "Dad has some fucking nerve showing that to you. He can be pissed off at me, but he had no right to upset you like that."

"Not only did I watch it, but apparently it was live streaming during your father's poker night."

"That's not possible," Morgan announced. "The only one who had access to that stream was the subscriber who requisitioned it."

"Yes, well. Let me unmask that subscriber for you, sweetheart." Melody grimaced.

"Dad?" Jamison looked pale.

"No. Not your father. Phillip."

"Who's Phillip?" Morgan asked, looking at Melody and then at Jamison

"My Dad's partner," Jamison addressed Morgan. He then turned to his mother. "Let me be sure I've go this right. Dad goes over to Phillip's for 'Poker Night,' and during a hand of cards they all choose to live stream a sex act? Please tell me you aren't buying this, Mom?"

"I trust your father, Jamison. And if he says it was Poker Night, then it was."

"You can't possibly be this naïve. Not after last time. How many chances is he gonna get? How many free passes?" Jamison questioned angrily.

"I will not have this conversation here," Melody stated, her distress evident on her face.

"You don't want to have this conversation here and yet, you thought it was a good idea to show up here, where I work, and have the conversation you started with me?"

"You have no right to be angry at me for just trying to be

protective of my son."

"Mom, I am a grown man and if what I am doing is a mistake, then it's my mistake to make. I will handle whatever consequences come with my actions. Just make sure you relay to dad that this is none of his concern," Jamison proclaimed. "I have to get to work," Jamison said, pushing past his mother and exiting the break room.

Melody called out after him, "This conversation is not over, young man!"

Morgan stood awkwardly, leaned up against the counter, staring at her feet when Melody walked toward her. Her Louboutin's clicked as she slowly stepped the five feet separating them and when Morgan finally looked up, she came face to face with Jamison's mother.

The look on Melody's face was not anger, hatred, or disgust, as Morgan expected, but one of sorrow. A look of pain and pleading. "Please tell me what I saw is not who he has become?"

"I don't think I understand the question you're asking me?" Morgan admitted.

"The behavior I saw from my son in that video. Please tell me the hurt and angry man who was rough, forceful, and dominating, is not who my son has become? I did my best, and I know I failed in so many ways, but please tell me I did not raise a monster whose only goal is to cause pain and do as he pleases with a woman?" She sucked in a deep breath and raised her shoulders as her body shuddered.

"Mrs. Masters, I can see there is something more going on here than just disappointment about a video. I'm not sure who your son is. It's like I said, I barely know him. But the torment written on your face is definitely something that warrants a conversation with someone more equipped to handle it than me. There are professionals more adept at having this conversation with you. And if there is a legitimate concern about whether it's just a kink, or if it's something more, then perhaps that's a conversation for you, your son, and the professional of your choice," Morgan stated.

Morgan began walking away, but before she turned the corner, she stopped. She looked back at Melody and said, "But for what it's worth, he didn't hurt me. Not really. And if he had tried to do something I wasn't okay with, I would have said something. Considering the scene, he was incredibly gentle. And he wasn't only doing things to please himself. As awkward as it is to have this conversation with you, I liked it. He was picking up on my needs and somehow read into what I wanted. So no, I don't think you raised a monster. I just think his appetite is a little more varied than what you might expect."

Morgan made her way to her office, but couldn't get Melody's words out of her head. *It's never just sex.* But it was. For Morgan, it was just sex. Sure, Kent and Lucas were fun, and she enjoyed spending time with them, but she was not looking for a relationship.

I need a boyfriend like I need a hole in the head, Morgan thought, chuckling to herself.

As she sat at her desk an hour later, getting ready to open her emails, a knock came at the door.

"Enter," she called out. She didn't look up from her computer to see who entered, but heard footsteps and then someone plopping down on one of her cushy chairs positioned in the room's corner.

"Sorry about all that," Jamison's husky voice called out to her from across the room where he sat twirling his pen.

She looked up, and they made eye contact. "What can I do for you, Mr. Masters?" Morgan asked.

"Really? I know you don't like me, but please don't call me that. Mr. Masters is my father. And I am nothing like that asshole."

"Are you one hundred percent certain about that?" Morgan teased, grinning from behind her computer screen as she sat scanning her inbox.

"Yes. I am certain of that," he said, rising from his chair and walking across the room. He stood at the left edge of Morgan's desk as she turned in her chair to face him.

"Well, then maybe I misjudged you." She giggled. "It doesn't happen often, but I have been wrong before. Do me a favor, though. Don't tell anyone, huh? I have a reputation to uphold."

"Speaking of that," Jamison asked, taking a seat on the corner of her desk. "Any plans for how you plan on dealing with the whole Phillip situation?"

"Phillip? Oh, yes. Your dad's partner and my ever so generous benefactor." Morgan grinned. "And what situation is it you think I need to deal with?"

"The video? The live stream? Ringing a bell?"

"Yes. I know what you're talking about. I was there, remember?"

"And?"

"And what, Jamison? There is nothing to do. He commissioned a project. One he paid handsomely for, I might add. You got your cut, so I don't see the issue."

"This wasn't a onetime live stream for his pleasure only, Morgan. That asshole live streamed it to a house full of people. And let me be clear, it was not fucking 'Poker Night.' Then he recorded and distributed it. Don't think that was in the original contract now, was it?"

"No, it specifically stated for personal use."

"Exactly. So, to me, it looks like you have a breach of contract here. All you have to do is threaten to sue him over it and he will settle out of court. Then that handsome payment we received will look like chump change."

"Are you suggesting I blackmail him for more money?"

"No. Huh uh. I suggest you make a prudent business decision and force that asshole to take you seriously. Make him treat you as the businesswoman you are. Seeing as this is your business," he said, pointing at Morgan.

"Why do you care?"

"I don't. Not really. I just hate that men like him and my dad get to keep treating women like shit and get away with it."

"A sensitive side. Who knew?" Morgan chuckled.

"And another thing..."

"What?" Morgan asked, a quizzical look replacing her smile as concern set in.

"Thank you."

"For what?"

"For the way you handled my mom. I overheard what she asked you. Let me just say that I appreciate your response."

"I said nothing I didn't actually believe."

"Well, regardless. You didn't have to. It's like you said. It's not like you even like me." He looked uncomfortable.

"Hold on a minute, did me saying that hurt the feelings of 'The' Jamison Masters?" Morgan teased as she stood up from her chair in front of him.

As she stood there looking at him, she saw something in his eyes, something just beneath the surface he was trying ever so hard to hide; his attraction to her radiated off of him. His pheromones and posture told the story his lips refused to tell.

Jamison grabbed Morgan by her elbow and spun her around.

He pressed her back against her desk as she stared up into his face with fear.

"Just what in the hell do you think you're doing?" she asked.

"Shut up," he said, grabbing underneath both of her thighs and lifting her onto her desk.

"Are you crazy?" she whispered.

"Relax. The door's locked," he said, trailing the back of his hand up her bare thigh toward the bottom edge of her skirt. "Tell me to stop," he commanded.

"And why on earth would I do that?" Morgan asked, smirking as she leaned back on her elbows, spreading her legs apart as Jamison looked down at her.

"Last chance," he said, his hand running up her inner thigh before brushing across the crotch of her panties. He slid one finger under the fabric. "Tell me to stop."

"Not a chance," she challenged.

Jamison quickly dropped to his knees in front of Morgan, pulling her panties aside to expose the snack he was craving.

He slid his tongue expertly along her lips and sucked her clit gently between his teeth as he breathed her scent in deeply.

He paused, leaning his head away from her. "Tell me again how it's just sex." Jamison replaced his head between her legs and continued his assault on her clit.

"It's just sex," she exaggerated between the deep breaths his tongue was coaxing from her.

"Swear it."

"It's just sex," she moaned as she raised her hips to meet his face, grinding her pussy against his chin.

Morgan's thighs pressed tightly against Jamison's ears as he dug his nails into the fleshy bits underneath them.

Jamison traced his name along her lips. First as if scribbling the letters on a page, reckless and messy as he drew the moisture from her, and then in cursive, taking his time and lining each letter accurately to draw the most of her sweetness onto his tongue for him to savor.

"You taste so fucking good," he said into her pussy. He paused, placing delicate kisses all around her opening before burying his face even further between her folds.

Jamison ran the tip of his nose along the most sensitive parts of her, adding pressure, then friction as she struggled to hold in her cries.

Hearing Morgan's attempts to muffle the sounds of the pleasure he was delivering, Jamison stopped.

"What... what are you doing? Wait! Where are you going?" Morgan pouted as Jamison rose to his feet and walked over to the loveseat in the center of the room.

He grabbed one of the accent pillows and tossed it to Morgan.

Sitting atop her desk with her skirt around her waist, and everything below it exposed, she caught the pillow.

"That should help," he said as he walked back to her. He grabbed the hand holding the pillow and raised it to her face. "Now, where was I?"

Jamison leaned over and slid one finger deep within her. He traced her insides with that one finger, spreading her wetness from one corner to the other, before allowing another finger to enter slowly.

Once both fingers were inside of her, he made small circles just at her entrance, waiting for the sensation to build. He had her just at the edge and wanting more. Craving more.

Biting down on that pillow, she arched her back, pressing herself farther onto his fingers. She scooted forward towards him, lifting and grinding onto his hand as she felt her climax building.

She was right there. He had her right there. And just when she was about to explode, he withdrew his fingers.

Jamison once again grabbed Morgan by her thighs, but this time he flipped her over, bending her over the desk.

He quickly undid his belt and slid his pants down over his ass. Then, reaching between her thighs, he covered his palm with her juices before rubbing them down the length of his cock.

Placing himself at her opening, he grabbed her by the back of her neck, pulling her up to him where he groaned into her ear, "I am going to make you cum all over my dick, and after I'm done, I'll shove my cock so far down your throat as I watch you taste yourself off of me."

Morgan whimpered with anticipation, and then Jamison took both of her arms, pinning them behind her, before he slammed his cock deep inside of her. There was no more muffling her cries. There was no way she could reach the pillow that had tumbled off her desk and landed on the floor at their feet. Her moans would reach someone's ears, but under no circumstances was Morgan going to stop him now.

She would take his punishment and ride his cock as he drew every ounce of satisfaction she could muster from her. And when she was done, the evidence of a job well done dripping down both their legs and coating his dick, she would kneel before him and draw his cock into her mouth.

She would feast on her satisfaction until his burst forth, allowing him to release all his anger and frustration into the back of her throat. And when he was done, she would smack his ass and send him back to work because, it's like she said, *it's just sex.*

About Last Time

The Morgan Ericksson Series

Book 2

ANGELA M. JOHNSON

ABOUT THE AUTHOR

Angela M. Johnson is BIPOC author of adult fantasy and romance living in Northwest Arkansas (NWA) with her family. She is active in her local writing community, encouraging aspiring authors by donating her time to educate and share her knowledge of resources. She is a retired Army Veteran, mother, artist, cosplayer, crafter, and Heavy Athlete competing in Scottish Highland Games. When she isn't writing, she is chasing dopamine by collecting skills and hobbies like they are Pokémon cards. Everything from digital illustration/design, 3D printing, laser engraving, CNC carving, and other types of fabrication. As an author, she takes the imagery playing in her mind as if from a streaming service, and delivers it in written form by way of epic adventures, comedic banter, romantic entanglements, and high stakes action. She published her first fantasy novel in 2022 and has now ventured into the romance genre; releasing four novels in 2023, one in 2025, and more to come in the future.